Hearts on Fire

LIA MICHAELS

Lia Michaels

ISBN: **1722390859**
ISBN-13: **978-1722390853**

DEDICATION

This book is dedicated to all those who have found their second chance for love. Grab on with both hands this time and never let it go. Trust in your heart and in the magic that is love.

CONTENTS

ACKNOWLEDGMENTS

Hearts on Fire turned out to be the story I needed to write at this time. It helped me explore the paranormal and magical worlds I had included in some of my previous books under my other pen names. Working on the Wildfire Romance shared world books, I found that my "thing" is writing paranormal stories. From witches to shifters to my favorite Gods and Goddesses, I want to have them in each story. They're a big part of my real life so why not put them in my fantasy worlds as well?

Without the whip cracking and patience of my friend, fellow author and editor, Amber Lea Easton I wouldn't have taken up this project. Her enthusiasm helped bring me out of a dark place and back into writing again. We drove each other bonkers, shed a lot of tears and tossed back a bottle or three of tequila to get these books out. Because she never gave up on me even when I gave up on myself, I will be forever grateful. She is one of my heart and soul sisters now and forever. Love you, girlie!

To my husband, whose name I scrambled to come up with this pen name, I give my heart now, forever and always. He stuck by me when I thought all was lost. He held my hand when I was too scared to take another step. He gave me hope and the will to live again. He is the real person behind my fantasy hubby Tony and gets a kick out of being a French bear shifter and "married" to four published authors. He was my second chance for love and now he's my always and forever.

I can't ask for more than that. I love you, Michael Liam Smith.

.

Chapter 1

Danielle Carson hung her leather jacket on the overcrowded coatrack and skirted around the three screaming brats racing around the reception area. She had scheduled this appointment with her favorite stylist over a month ago in order to avoid this sort of thing. Unfortunately, school had been cancelled due to another bomb threat. Now a sea of the minions accompanied their frazzled parents all over town. Thankfully, she wouldn't have much longer to wait to be escorted back to the private workstation of one of her best friends.

"Faye is running a couple minutes behind, but I'll tell her you're here. You want your usual?"

"I'll take the loaded stuff this time. I'm going to need it." She tilted her head in the direction of the two rug rats in the corner crawling under the oversized chairs.

Cameron rolled his eyes and smiled. "You and me both, sister! Coke extra ice coming right up."

One of the salon assistants busied herself lowering the blinds of the windows. The weatherman had predicted an overcast day but the sun had other plans. The blinding light had done nothing to help the pounding in her brain. At least the blinds gave her a bit of a reprieve.

She glanced around the room and took in the new décor. Life sized photos of the salon's celebrity clientele now graced the wall behind the beverage station. The rest of the room had been remodeled in various shades of teal and black. She slid her palm along the armrest of the chair she occupied and sighed. No faux leather for this joint. Thankfully the mother of the rowdy bunch kept them off the furniture.

Danielle hummed along with the Melissa Etheridge tune coming through the speakers hidden within the artwork throughout the room. The deep raspy voice had always been one of her favorites and one more sign she needed to be in the salon at that moment in time.

She craned her neck to see what kept Cameron and her drink. Normally she would ask for one of their lemon or cucumber water concoctions but the headache creeping over her temples demanded the caffeine. She wasn't a coffee person and preferred her own special collection of loose-leaf teas to anything they would be able to brew in the shop. Thankfully, the salon owners keep the favorites of their regulars on hand. It's one of the many reasons she kept coming in every month.

And to spend the afternoon with her soul sister, Faye.

No one else on the planet understood Danielle's restlessness more than her friend and confidant. Whenever her spirit needed a reboot, Faye would drop everything to be by her side. Today happened to be one of those days.

"Give me back my book! Mahhhhhm!"

The shrill tone of the girl in pigtails pierced through her skull. *Now you've done it, short stuff.*

Her fingers tingled as the power surged through her. She rolled her head on her shoulders, closed her eyes, and recited the spell.

"Noisy children running amok, should all sit down and read a book. Inside voices and quiet feet will soon be rewarded with their favorite treat."

She repeated the incantation three times, opened her eyes and closed the spell. "So mote it be."

One by one, the children picked out books from their backpacks and settled down into the chairs close to the windows. She smiled and glanced up as Cameron stood in front of her with her drink, his mouth open.

"You did that thing you do, didn't you?"

"Maybe. Are you complaining? I can reverse it if you wish." Her eyes held his and dared him to say he preferred the caterwauling over the peace.

"Gurrrrl. I was going to ask you if you wanted a job here."

"Don't you have phones to answer, Cameron?" Faye's low sultry voice caused the receptionist to spin on his heels and dive back behind the desk.

He snapped the phone headset over the top of his head without missing a beat. "Teasin' and Pleasin' Salon. How can we rock your world today?"

She laughed and stood to fold herself into the arms of the statuesque red head. "Don't be mad with him. He knew better to interrupt me in the middle of my thing."

Faye rolled her eyes. "I was about to make the shop a no kid zone, but thanks to you I don't have to suffer the wrath of my partners. Customer is always right and all that crap."

She followed her friend through the dozen occupied workstations toward the offices in the back. "I wasn't sure it was going to work. I haven't been sleeping well and these headaches have thrown me off my game."

"Well, what did you expect? That bitch broke up with you through Facebook. She didn't even have the decency to tell you to your face. You should be using voodoo on her and that has-been she's shacking up with now."

She sighed and plopped down in the chair at the hair washing station. Her relationship with Amy had been a hot mess from the get go. She wasn't ever *in* love with the other woman but had cared deeply for her. As much as she wanted to say she saw this coming, it still hurt like hell to have the person who claimed to love you for over two years toss you aside. She could understand it to some extent if it had been with someone in their circle, but not this bozo.

"Honestly, the on again off again bullshit between us had become exhausting. If she wants to be the latest in a long line of broads who've fallen for the douche, who am I to stop her?"

"I'll give her credit for one thing. She never hid her obsession with Dylan. It's not your fault you got caught up in the middle of those two. He loved having a groupie who would do anything for him, including bedding one of the owners of the hottest resort in Nevada."

"She kept begging me to use my influence to get his band a slot in the eighties' rival tour. She was pissed when I refused. Break up number one happened right after that argument."

"That should've been the end of it right there."

She smirked. "What can I say? When it was good between us, the sex was fucking hot."

Faye laughed. "Okay, that's two things I'll give her credit for with you. Too bad she wouldn't give up on bagging a rock star."

"Personally, I don't see the charm of a leather clad singer well past his prime. Give me someone like Jon Bon Jovi or Kip Winger and I'd be all over him. Their talent only improved as they got older."

"You gotta have talent in order for it to age at all. Amy has only ever had one talent and that has been spreading her legs for third rate tone deaf musicians."

"Oh snap! You got that right. Neither of them can't carry a tune."

Their laughter lightened her mood and raised her spirits. This had been exactly what she needed after a night of tossing and turning. The dreams came to her in frantic jumbles of images, flashes of her past, present and future. In every one she ran toward beings who had always been with her, through each rebirth and renewal. This time seemed different. She had to reunite with them now.

The balance between the various magical realms had always been tenuous at best, but something huge headed their way. Someone, or something blocked her from seeing it and it pissed her off.

She focused her attention back on their conversation. Faye hadn't appeared to notice she had drifted into her own thoughts, but Danielle knew better. The two of them had always been able to pick up on each other's moods. This time, Faye assumed her mind continued to be on Amy.

Faye pulled a stack of dark teal towels and matching smocks from the cabinet. "If she has the nerve to show her face around here again, I'm going to rip out those sorry ass extensions of hers. No one humiliates my boo like that and lives to tell about it."

Danielle laughed. "Thanks, Faye Rae. Nice to know you always have my back."

"Twenty-four seven, doll face. I damn near choked on my Moscato when that sleazy photo of her showed up in my feed. Little Miss White Trash had herself pinned against a door with that asshole's tongue tickling her tonsils. To rub salt in your wounds they slapped on the 'just married' hashtag. You know that was staged, right?"

"Amy is crass but that's not her style."

"Not her. Him. Dylan Sheldon won't accept his glory days are long over. This is his way to keep his mug all over the Internet. The two of them deserve each other. When this falls apart, and you know it will, don't you dare take her back. She zapped the life out of you whenever she was around."

She crossed her heart and held up her hand with her pinky finger out. "I swear."

Faye's expertly manicured finger hooked with hers. "I hope you tossed all of her shit out on the street. Let the bums have it."

She grinned and helped Faye cover the table next to them with the beautician's tools and bottles of hair dye. "I donated everything to Goodwill."

Faye tilted her head back and laughed. She had to hold onto the edge of the table until she was able to speak again. She draped one of the smocks over her and fastened the snaps behind her neck. "Now that's my Dani! Are we going to do your usual or change it up?"

She removed the clip holding her hair in place and pulled her fingers through her shoulder length curls. "Chop it off. I want spikes and sass."

Faye's eyes stared into hers in the mirror in front of them. "Don't tease me. You know I've wanted to do that for you since I got my license."

She nodded. "I'm serious. I want a makeover to match how I'm feeling. Grab the colors too. I want pink and purple streaks."

Faye combed her fingers through her hair as she mulled over Danielle's request and visualized the end result. "I'll have to bleach the hell out of your hair for the color to take, but if we strategically place the streaks, they'll pop against your dark chestnut."

She grinned. "I knew I could count on you to visualize what I wanted."

Faye kissed her cheek. "You're not fooling anyone, love. You've been sending out pictures to my head since last night. Your magic feels sad. If this brings you to a happier place, then you can be damn sure I'm going to do it."

She closed her eyes to ease the sting of impending tears. She had sworn to herself she wouldn't break down, but with Mercury still in retrograde, she didn't have a chance. Her emotions controlled her magic and, right now, that made her dangerous not only to herself but to everyone around her. She had to get out of town and wait it out. She planned to discuss it all with her business partners that night. They had recently completed the construction and interior design of a new resort, bar and nightclub a few miles outside of Ouray, Colorado. The grand opening bad been planned for months and Danielle wanted to immerse herself in it.

Up until the fiasco with Amy, she had had no intention of ever leaving Nevada. Elko had been her home for most of her life, but now it had lost its appeal. The opportunity to start over with a clean slate had fallen in her lap and she decided to run with it. All she had to do now was convince her partners she needed to do this for herself as well as the success of their business expansion. The House of Taboo had taken off from the moment the doors opened. Within their first year, they had become the go to place for locals and celebrities from all over the world. A decade later, she had the chance to do the same for the sleepy town along the famous Million Dollar Highway. Taboo II had been her baby from its conception, so why not make it official?

Ouray is rich in the magic of the Fae. I can feel it calling to me. If there is any place on earth I can find myself and the answers to the visions in my dreams, it's there.

*

Mark splashed water over his face and chastised himself for spending half the night slamming down tequila shots. The last of the booze burned out of his system leaving a solid pounding at his temples. As a pup on the force, he would be able to chug three or four bottles of Jose without skipping a beat. At fifty, he was lucky to get through a pitcher of beer before having to call it a night.

"I'm too old for this shit."

His partner, Ian, had warned him to take it easy. They had been on the road for a week and hadn't found a safe zone to run wild. He touched the image on his right forearm. Everyone in their pack had the same tattoo of a Navajo Warrior in front of a full moon. Only other shifters and their allies could see the image morph into a wolf with glowing eyes. While he didn't need the full moon to transform, it was the best time to repair and rejuvenate. Tonight, the phase would begin and it couldn't come fast enough for him.

"Feels like I fell from the roof and then ran over by a semi." He sat down at the table in the full-sized kitchen of their hotel room.

Ian handed him a mug of coffee, black. "You dove in front of it and slipped. Damn good thing you kept tumbling and hid in the alley. It took me ten minutes to convince the driver the dog he rolled over had run off and didn't appear to be injured. What the hell were you thinking, Mark?"

"I wasn't thinking. I thought I saw an injured woman in the street."

"The same one you've been dreaming about?" Ian's eyes clouded over with worry.

"I'm not losing it. I need to run. How much further do we have to go?"

Ian tossed his phone on the table so it slid into his hand. He tapped the button to wake up the screen. There in black and white was the confirmation for their flights out of southern California to Elko, Nevada. "Tony and Lia know we're coming?"

Ian nodded. "Who do you think arranged the flight? Tony has been chompin' at the bit to get us out there before the start of the full moon. He promised a safe place to rest, run and, of course, play."

He tilted his head toward the bedroom where the two girls slept. They had partied all night long, crawling from club to club until three. He vaguely remembered one of the chicks sucking him off before she had passed out cold. "What about them? I may still be a bit foggy but I recall you promising they could join us on the road."

"The room is paid in full through tomorrow morning, and the manager will make sure they're out of here well before then. I don't know about you, but I'm ready to start this new venture and maybe put down some roots. From what Lia has told me, Ouray could be the spot for us. Plus, we get to run a resort for our kind of people. No more hiding out in secret clubs. I want a place to call our own."

He wanted the same. That's one of the reasons he came up with for dreaming about the same woman all the time. Someone hurt her, someone she trusted and now she's running to find where she belongs. His heart is drawn to her, more like obsessed with having her in his world. Their pack leader in San Fran had told him that kind of attraction was only found between soul mates and, when a wolf finds his mate, nothing will keep them apart.

"Maybe this girl in your dreams will end up finding you in Colorado. Hell, maybe she'll be there when we stop off in Nevada. The House of Taboo is a popular spot."

"All right. All right. Let me grab my gear."

He prayed to Mother Moon to put him in the path of his dream girl. If she were the one he searched for, he and Ian would finally be able to leave the Nomadic life behind.

*

Ian gathered up the empty mugs and stacked them in the small dishwasher. He liked their current digs but the charm had worn off and he itched to be back on the road. His partner thought it was because he needed the adrenaline rush. Ian told him he had had enough of the palm trees, long-legged platinum blondes, with fake tits and asses. Truth was, Ian had been having the same dream, about the same woman. In his mind, she was to be their mate. In his dream world he saw the power around her. Right now, it was a raging storm. She, too, searched for her mate—the one to help her calm and focus her magic.

The one who placed his mark on her in another life so he could find her over and over again.

What if it's not one, but two? Mark is the ying to my yang in and out of the pack. Where one goes, the other follows. Period. Forever and ever, amen.

He knew without a doubt their dream woman was waiting for them. His wolf howled to be let free to find her and take her as their mate. Even though the desire raged through his veins, he wouldn't ever force her. She would have to choose them and their lifestyle. It would be the only way it would work.

He and Mark had shared partners before, last night's foursome had merely satisfied an itch. Nothing to ease the fire within him, but enough to help keep his beast inside. That's all he could hope for since they had lost their pack leader two years ago. His death had left a void that had to be filled, or the pack disbanded.

He and Mark chose to retire and let the rest of them fight it out.

Together they'd managed to save enough to be able to travel around the world again if they had wanted. Instead, they hit the road in his Mustang looking for adventure and more of their kind. No matter where they went, nothing clicked. He realized they no longer fit in with any of the other packs. The time had come for them to start their own.

*

"Don't get your thong in a bunch, Cameron. My girls are expecting me. I don't need your help to find my way."

Danielle snorted. "Right on time."

Every time her friend came around, Cameron turned into a flustered hot mess. Danielle really couldn't blame him, as she herself had been fangirling over the woman since the day they met. She wished he would learn to relax and not try so hard.

The door burst open to reveal who had caused all commotion. There she stood, larger than life and towering over Cameron in her sky-high heels. Lia Michaels whipped around and pinned the wide-eyed receptionist to the doorframe with only the expression on her face. "Dude, if you don't back off, I'm going to clock you with this bag of burgers and ruin our lunch. Trust me. You don't want get in the way of me and my food coma."

He opened his mouth to object and she swung the bag at his head.

Cameron screamed and clutched at the chains around his neck. "All right! The three of you crazy bitches are about to give me a nervous breakdown."

Lia stomped her foot in his direction and he bolted for the front of the salon. She turned and rewarded them with one of her most innocent looks. "That man needs to relax."

Faye liberated the food from Lia's clutches. "You know you scare the shit out of him, right?"

Lia blanched and dropped the rest of her things on the marble topped table next to the door. "That's my point. He really needs to get out more if I scare him."

Danielle laughed. "The one time he shows his face at Taboo, you choose to be dressed to the nines in your hot pink Dominatrix gear."

"No! It was the whip wasn't it? He freaked when he saw the whip. Most people do. It's badass."

Faye shook her head. "The boots. He's jealous they don't come in his size."

Their peals of laughter brought Cameron back. "I'll have you know I found them in my size. I damn near gave myself a concussion falling down a flight of stairs walking in them."

His confession triggered another round of laughter at his expense. They didn't mean to make fun of him, but he made it too damn easy.

He marched away from them again muttering. "You can all go to hell for all I care."

Lia pouted and rummaged through her purse. She yanked out her phone and punched the speed dial button. "Hey babe. Could you ask Dina whip up her lunch special and have it delivered to Cameron? Extra sauce the way he likes it? Perfect. Okay, lover. I'll tell them."

"Tell us what?" She dove into her fries with extra chili and cheese. She made a note to be sure this would be on the menu in Ouray.

"Tony sends his love and a reminder that he expects both of you to help him show his college buds a good time this weekend. Starting tonight."

Faye raised her hands. "Count me in."

"I really feel bad about Cam. All he had to do was ask and I would've given him lessons on how to bring out his inner Domme. Not my fault he's afraid to embrace her." She grabbed one of the tall stools from another station and distributed the rest of the food.

Faye sat down next to them and chuckled. "Never mind him. You got here in the nick of time. Boo is gonna let me chop off her curls."

Lia dropped her burger back onto its wrapper and narrowed her eyes. "Are you sure, or are you doing this to rebel against Airhead Amy?"

Her jaw clenched. She hated when Lia referred to Amy like that. Even now, after all she had put her through, Danielle had to bite down on the inside of her cheek to stop herself from defending her ex. "I want a clean slate and I thought a makeover would be a good place to start."

"And Ouray is next?"

"I know you said you have people in mind to run it, but I want Taboo II for my own. I'm not saying cut the others out, give me a chance to put it on the map. I designed every inch of that place and

handpicked the dude who did all the woodwork. You and Tony
teased me about spending months picking out the glassware alone."

Faye's eyes darted back and forth between them as she finished
off her burger. "If anyone can do it…"

Lia tossed her unruly mop of multicolored long hair over her
shoulder and grinned. "About time you came around, girl. Your
partners fly in tonight."

She choked on the fry she had in her mouth. "Tony's friends?"

"I'm sorry for not telling you sooner. Tony wanted the three of
you to meet without any preconceived notions. In order for Taboo II
to work, the chemistry between all of you has to be there from the
start. We've all invested a fortune in this venture and can't afford it to
fail."

"Then that's settled. You want the new resort to take off
running? No one else can make it happen." Faye gathered the empty
wrappers and busied herself setting up everything she needed to
create the look Danielle wanted.

"I have to say, I'm proud of you for changing things up. I don't
want to have you mooning over that broad when you could find
yourself in the middle of these studs. If they weren't Tony's best
friends…"

Faye raised her eyebrows as she mixed up the bleach agent.
"Don't you even joke about cheating on my boyfriend."

"You'll feel the same after you meet them. Trust me. Besides, it's
not cheating when your partner gives his blessing."

"Weren't you dating one of them before you met Tony?" She
swore Lia had told them the story of how all three men had
competed for her affections.

"Ian had been the one to approach me first. I was supposed to
be on a tour of the campus with other prospective freshmen. That
night, I'm at a frat party going hot and heavy with him. Next thing I
know, he's talked me into a threesome and in walks Antonin
Michaels."

Faye put her hands on her hips. "Roll it back, sister. Did you
have that threesome?"

Lia shook her head and her eyes sparkled with mischief. "Where
Ian goes, so does Mark."

She had known Lia and Tony had lead a polyamorous lifestyle
off and on during their marriage but had never thought it went back

to their college days in Michigan. Now that the information sank in she had to admit it made sense. There had to be great love and respect between them to remain friends for decades.

Faye fiddled with her iPod until satisfied she had found the perfect playlist starting off with Pink's "Raise Your Glass." Danielle smiled. Perfect song to kick off their afternoon and her new path.

"How did you know Tony was *the one?*"

"I dreamt about him. As soon as our eyes zeroed in on each other, I understood what all the hoopla about soul mates was about. Part of me had been missing and I didn't know it until he returned it."

"Mm...hmm. Sounds like a fairy tale to me. Enough chitchat. Hop back in the chair, boo. You're not the only one who can perform magic."

She smiled and did as she was told. The soft cushions molded to her body in all the right places and she relaxed for the first time in weeks. She closed her eyes and listened to her friends catch up on the local gossip and an adoring Cameron pledge his undying love for Lia's peace offering from Taboo's kitchen.

While she would miss moments like this, she had to follow the call to Ouray. The pull on her became stronger with each passing moon phase and used her dreams to show her the way to her soul mates. She recalled one of the last lessons she had with the Crone. She had said the White Witch and her Guardians would reunite in this lifetime as they had done in every one before now. The elderly witch had told her it would be after a time of great turmoil and upheaval in their lives, during the first full moon to herald new beginnings.

Tomorrow would be the first full moon of the new year...

The Wolf Moon.

Chapter 2

"Mark! Help me!"

His heart raced as the panic rose to a fever pitch. With every scream a part of him died. "I'm coming! Please hold on, my love."

"They're tearing me apart. I can't fight them any longer…"

"No!"

Please don't leave me again. I don't want to live another life without you. Please…

"Mark! Help me!"

His body jumped and the dream faded. His eyes darted around taking in his surroundings. Ian slumped against the window in the seat next to him, fast asleep. He caught the eye of the perky flight attendant. She smiled and brought him the bottle of water he had asked for when she had made the rounds before he dozed off. He chugged down half of it and set it aside as he unbuckled his seatbelt. Even though Tony had managed to book their seats in first class, his body still had cramped up sitting in one position for over an hour. He stood and stretched, his eyes never stopping their constant surveillance of his surroundings.

Old habits may die hard, but they tended to keep him and Ian alive and out of trouble. If only they would carry over into his dreams about the girl. The one who screamed for him to find her.

The one he called his love.

A chime rang out over the plane's intercom.

"We're now making our final approach for the Elko Regional Airport. Passengers please take your seats and prepare for landing."

He sat down and fastened his seat belt again. "Ian?"

"Wha…?" He turned his head toward him and opened one eye.

"We're about to land."

"Of course, we are. I swear the universe is against me. I was about to rock the world of a very appreciative flight attendant."

A gasp followed by a round of giggles reached his ears. "Wanna trade dreams?"

Ian shrugged. "Dreams are never as good as the real thing, brotha. I hate to see you this tore up over someone who may not exist."

"I didn't ask for these nightmares."

"That's not what I meant. Run them by Lia and see if she can make sense out of them. As soon as we get settled in Ouray, we can reach out to Shaman. Maybe the prophecy has changed."

He closed his eyes as their plane descended and brought them one step closer to the next phase of their new life. Mark trusted Ian's instincts in everything else, but not with the dreams.

Every time they had been able to check in with Shaman, the visions had always remained the same. His mate had been intentionally hidden from him and he'd be damned if whoever did this would get away with it.

Ian lifted his chin toward the end of the chaotic baggage claim area as he pulled the last of his luggage from the carousel. "He hasn't changed a bit."

He laughed. "Being married to Lia would keep anyone forever young."

Ian scanned the crowd. "Looks like he's flying solo this afternoon."

"I wouldn't be so sure about that."

He focused on the sliding glass doors behind Tony. The sky had begun to shift from blue to the brilliant reddish hue of sunset, and the perfect backdrop for their welcoming committee. He held his breath as the subject of their conversation sashayed toward them. Her rainbow-colored hair piled high on her head and cascading down her back. Her open trench coat billowed behind her like a cape exposing her leather-covered curves.

The woman knew how to make an entrance.

Ian braced himself as she launched into his arms. He spun her around and kissed her soundly on the lips. "For a moment there, I thought you skipped out on us."

"Not on your life, Stud Muffin."

Mark tapped him on the shoulder. "What about me?"

"Saving the best for last, mon amour." She kissed both of his cheeks.

He held her close as he slowly bent her backward. He planted a kiss at the base of her throat.

Her bawdy laughter echoed throughout the room and brought smiles to the faces of everyone around them, including her husband.

Tony pulled Ian into a bear hug. "It's about damn time you made it out here."

"You know how it is, brotha. Had to burn off a little steam before putting down roots."

Mark smiled. "More like sober up!"

Tony yanked Mark into a headlock. "You're lucky I love you like a brother otherwise I'd be jealous as hell you can make my wife laugh like that."

Lia adjusted her cleavage and linked her arm through Tony's. "He can make me laugh, but only you can rock my world."

His heart ached to have that kind of love, one wild and free.

She's out there. We can feel her.

Black Wolf and me.

Tony tipped his head toward the exit. "Your chariot awaits, along with a fully stocked bar."

Ian grasped his shoulder. "You always knew how to get the party started. Wouldn't think you had it in ya this time of year."

Tony grinned. "Man, I've missed you, hibernation jokes and all."

The two of them walked ahead with their luggage. He hung back and offered his arm to Lia.

"What's wrong, Mark? You're not yourself. Don't try to tell me you're fine. I know a restless soul when I see it."

He kissed her cheek. "Nothing the Moon and time with the two of you won't fix."

"If it's within my power to bring that megawatt smile back, I'll do it. No questions asked."

A shrill whistle drew his attention away from her violet eyes. Ian and Tony appeared to have the car loaded and were ready to take off.

LIA MICHAELS

Twilight had snuck up on them as the last of the sun's rays sunk below the horizon. "I'll keep that in mind."

He held her hand as she stepped into the back of the limo and slid over to make room for the rest of them. The soft leather seats cushioned his aching frame. After over three hours in flight, he had enough of tight spaces. Their current transportation was a welcome reprieve. He stretched out his legs, put his hands behind his head and sighed.

Ian laughed and took the open bottle of beer Tony handed to him. "Give him five minutes and he'll be snoring."

Mark grinned and drank from his own beer. "You're just jealous."

Lia kicked off her boots and folded her legs under her. She settled back against the cushions and her husband of over two decades. "You've got nothing on my teddy bear here."

Tony smiled and took their friendly ribbing in stride. "What do you think about the pale ale?"

"Is this from the brewery in Ouray?" Ian spun the label around to check out the logo.

Tony nodded. "High Altitude Brewing Company run by Darby Shaw. I had her ship us a couple cases to try out right before we offer it here on tap. If you agree, it will be one Taboo II will feature as well."

He filled his mouth with the beer and let the cold liquid slide over his tongue and down his throat. The subtle flavor reminded him of the traditional British pale ales but also the brasher hops used in the American versions. "I'd say Ms. Shaw nailed this recipe. It's the perfect blend."

Ian agreed. "After the fruity craze in the San Fran microbrews, I almost gave up on finding one that grabbed my taste buds again. This one does it in spades."

"Excellent. Dani raved about it last night as well."

His interest piqued. "Who?"

Tony leaned forward and rested his forearms on his thighs. "You'll meet her tonight. She's your third partner and will be moving to Ouray with the two of you."

Ian rubbed his hand over his jaw. "Sorry. Did you say 'she'?"

"What's the matter? You have something against working with a woman?" Lia's eyes narrowed and she appeared ready to pounce.

18

"No, darlin'. I'm a little surprised is all. The two of you never mentioned her name before now. I guess I assumed we'd be working with—"

"Someone like us." He finished Ian's sentence without a second thought. He knew he didn't have to elaborate.

Tony lifted an eyebrow. "Is that all? Do you think we'd partner you up with someone who's clueless about our world?"

Ian shrugged. "No, but even if you did it wouldn't be a problem to adjust. We've worked with humans before, but it's a hell of a lot easier to avoid any problems and stick with our kind. You know, those with ties to one of the magical realms."

Lia scrolled through the photos on her phone. "You have nothing to worry about on that front. Here. You tell me what you see."

Mark took the phone and gasped. Bursts of fire and ice shot up and down his spine. He fought to give voice to all of his emotions raging war within his body. Love, lust, anticipation and fear of the unknown, joy, surprise and relief to find he wasn't crazy after all.

Ian snatched the phone from his hands. "What the hell has you so spooked?"

"Look. At. Her."

Ian's biceps bulged as he clenched and unclenched his fist. He handed the phone back to Lia and wiped his palms over his jeans. His eyes bore into Mark's and he spoke to him through their minds.

"It's her. She's the one you've been dreaming about. She's been right under our noses all this time."

"The Prophesy. It's about us? What the hell, Ian?"

"Hey! Use your words, boys. You don't keep secrets from your family." Lia crossed her arms over her chest. Her eyes darted between the two of them and back to Tony.

Mark raked through his hair with his fingers. He struggled to find the words to explain but nothing sounded right. He thought it best to come clean with all of it now as the full moon phased peaked tomorrow night. If Danielle was truly who he had been searching for, Black Wolf would demand to be with her and so would Ian's Gray.

"I've been dreaming about her for months now. That's not entirely true. I've dreamed about her my entire life. It was six months

19

ago that her face was revealed to me. I didn't know who she was; only that someone she trusted hurt her. She's running and calling out to me."

Ian bumped his shoulder against his. "You're not alone. She's in my dreams as well."

"Christ, Ee. You could've told me before now. I thought Shaman had it wrong. He's been talking about us since the beginning."

"Wait. Both of you have been dreaming about our Dani?" Lia gripped Tony's hand resting on her thigh.

Mark nodded. "Her hair is different in my dreams but I would know those eyes anywhere."

"Answer me true, doll face. Does Dani know she's a witch with Fae blood?" Ian's voice took on the good cop tone he had used to interrogate suspects in the past.

"Since birth. Her grandmother gave her that much about her heritage. She never approved of Dani pursuing her calling and did everything she could to interfere with it. Her grandfather is no better.

"She hasn't had any formal training, then?" He wondered how she could possibly be the most powerful witch in history with her background. None of it jibed with what the dreams had been telling them.

Lia nodded. "She's a solitary, but an elderly woman took her back under her wing around the time we met her for the first time, fifteen years ago." She turned to her husband for confirmation.

"Give or take a couple years."

Ian pursued his line of questioning. "She have a tattoo on her hip that looks like a circle with a Celtic symbol associated with it?"

She nodded. "Full moon with the Trinity Knot. One on each hip."

Mark sat back stunned. "Two tats? Did she happen to have scars or birth marks that she covered with the ink?"

"She never mentioned that. She's had both tattoos for as long as we've known her."

Tony tapped Lia's phone. "Don't you have a picture of them?"

"Oh shit! I forgot. Hang on." Her nails clicked with lightning speed through her folders until she found the photo. She placed the phone back into Mark's hands.

Ian leaned in close as Mark enlarged the image. "That's it."

The limo turned onto the drive leading up to the House of Taboo. In his mind he had pictured something more on the lines of the casinos in Vegas with the bright lights and glaring neon signs. This was more to his tastes, subtle and yet vibrant. Elegant and classy without the cheesy Hollywood nonsense they left behind in California.

Mark turned his eyes back to the phone and traced over the tattoo design with his fingertip. He calmed his Wolf and pleaded with it to give them more time to be sure Dani was their chosen.

"Shaman said our mates would have these markings. We assumed the vision showed him two separate people. Never thought he meant the tattoos would be on the one woman who could unite the Fae and the Wolves. The one known as the White Witch."

Chapter 3

"Mighty fine of your partners to send up some champs to celebrate." Faye handed her the card that came with the bottle. She smiled and she read the note.

New venture. New life. New Beginnings.
Can't wait to jump into it all with you.

Until tonight,

Mark and Ian

Faye tapped the label. "Pommery Brut Royal is your favorite. You need to bring you're A-game tonight, Boo. Knock their socks off and they'll be putty in your hands."

"We'll work on the putty part later. I simply want to kick back, relax and let Mother Moon work her magic."

She popped open the bottle and inhaled. The delicate citrus and berry undertones tantalized her senses and broke open one of the barriers in her mind. The faces of the beings in her dreams came into focus and then morphed into wolves. One black as night, and the other dark brown and smoky gray. Both with eyes reflecting the light of the moon.

Faye's hand covered hers. "What did you see?"

"My future." She poured the bubbly into the glasses she had placed on top of the bar.

"I know that look. You don't need to protect me. I can take it."

She realized her friend must think the worst. "I'm not protecting you from anything. When I'm sure of what my dreams and visions are telling me, you'll be one of the first to know. I trust you with my life, Faye. Always have and always will. That's why I wanted to have you stay with me this weekend. Can't have a kickass Full Moon ritual without both of my soul sisters."

"This ritual wouldn't happen to involve all of us getting naked would it? I had a full body wax in case." Faye raised her eyebrows up and down.

She handed her one of the glasses of champagne and laughed. "I promised you a kick ass ritual, didn't I? Stripping will be an integral part if I have anything to say about it. Since I'm the one performing the ceremony, I'd say it's a done deal. Come on, let's get you settled in your room. I need your help. I have a full closet and absolutely no idea what to wear tonight."

Faye grabbed her bags and waved her along. "Give me five minutes to hang up my things and then I'll complete your transformation. If you don't have what I picture in my head, we can always raid Lia's closets!"

She kicked off her sneakers and stripped out of her clothes as she moved through her room. She caught her reflection in the mirror and brought her hands up to touch her hair. The pink and purple really did pop as Faye had promised. She shook her head and giggled at the way her hair flipped around. Even messy, the cut gave her the boost of confidence she'd needed to break free of the rut she'd been in. She had stopped trusting in herself and her magic had suffered.

Danielle stood naked and barefoot in her closet, debating on what to wear to best show off her new do. She wanted all eyes to be on her embracing her future. Their regulars and new guests all demanded she provide them with the experience they had come to expect from House of Taboo, no matter what chaos swirled around her personal life. She would insist upon the same if their roles were reversed.

"I have to say, I love your digs here over your apartment. You have so much more room. The guest suite is da bomb and don't get me started on this closet of yours." Faye smiled and sipped from her glass of champagne

"No point in renewing the lease after Amy left. This has always been my home away from home."

"And away from Amy?"

She nodded. "I don't have to keep going through the motions as someone I'm not. The haircut is only the beginning. You know you're my inspiration, right?"

Faye sat her glass down on the dressing table in the center of the room and embraced her. "You, Lia and Tony helped bring out the real me. Without you, I would never have made it through all of my surgeries. I inspire you? Boo, you're the reason I'm alive today."

Tears welled up in her eyes. "I'm going to miss the hell out of you."

Faye hugged her tighter. "Ditto. I might follow you out there. I have to make sure these new partners of yours treat you right."

"I would expect nothing less and I'm going to pester the hell out of you until you do."

Faye dabbed at her eyes. "Now you've gone and made me muck up my makeup. You pour yourself into that black halter mini dress and pair it up with your patent leather thigh-highs while I fix my face. In that outfit, you'll have everyone eating out of the palm of your hands."

"I haven't been with a man in ages. I don't want to make a fool of myself."

"Honey, as soon as his lips are on yours, it will all come back to you. That's the beauty of being single. You get to love the one you're with or jump on into a ménage party. Isn't that what you encourage here? Kink of all flavors and sizes?"

She laughed. "Touché."

The dull thud of a door closing reached her ears followed by the clack, clack, clack of heels on hard wood floors. "What the hell is keeping the two of you? The guys are already four rounds of shots ahead of us."

Lia smiled and ogled her appearance. "My vote is to head down as you are. Maybe keep the boots?"

She shook her head and stepped into the halter dress. It fit every curve and left nothing to the imagination. She wouldn't dream of ruining the effect with adding lingerie underneath, not even the floss fashionistas call thongs. "You've seen me naked a gazillion times. What are you staring at?"

"Your moons. They're glowing."

She grabbed the hem of her skirt and lifted it to expose her right hip, then her left. "What the fuck? That's never happened before."

"They weren't glowing an hour ago. That's new." Faye touched the ink and yanked her fingers away.

She flattened her palms and covered both of her moon tattoos and didn't feel anything. "What happened? Did I hurt you?"

"You gave me a zap, like grabbing a live wire." She held her fingers up to show a red burn that faded away to nothing before their eyes.

"Why is this happening to me now? The peak isn't until tomorrow night."

The air around her crackled with the raw electricity she thought she would never experience again. Not since before Amy dropped into her life. Now with the Wolf Moon approaching, Danielle's spirit broke free from the binding spell that had held it in check.

"Welcome back, dear heart. Time to claim your mates and return home"
She recognized the voice in her head. *"Nanny Rowan?"*
"Come home, child. You'll find the answers to all of your questions here."

She opened her mind to the psychic energy swirling around her. Songs, spells, traditions of her people and memories of her life before she was sent to live with her grandparents flowed through her. Wave after wave washed over her heart and soul.

The path before her became crystal clear.

Lia and Faye stood in front of her, their eyes filled with wonder at her full transformation.

The magic of her ancestors had returned to its rightful heir.

*

Ian stacked another shot glass on top of those he had emptied and waved off the refill. The hot little number behind the bar licked her lips and made sure he appreciated the full view of her tits spilling out over her dark pink and black corset. He groaned and adjusted his jeans to accommodate his growing cock.

So much eye candy and not enough time for him to sample it all.

"*Mon dieu.*" Tony stood up from his chair and reached out his hand. He appeared stunned by what he had witnessed.

He turned to see who had approached their table. He slapped Mark's chest with the back of his hand to get his attention away from the waitress and focused on the vision standing in front of them. He pushed up from his chair and had to hold onto the table to steady his legs.

Gray Wolf panted and howled to be set free.

Mark stood and offered her his chair.

Danielle tilted her head to the side. Her eyes drank both of them in from head to toe and smiled. "I'm sorry to have kept you waiting. Welcome to the House of Taboo."

He offered his chair to the honey-skinned redhead. Her scent alone spiked his arousal off the charts. With three beauties at their table, he didn't have a chance.

Tony signaled to the bar to bring over another round of tequila. "Danielle, my love. I've never seen you so—"

"Smokin'." Faye winked and placed her hand on Ian's thigh.

His cock strained against the confines of his jeans.

"Delicious." Lia blew her a kiss.

"Magnifique." Tony brought her hand to his lips.

Danielle's cheeks blushed. "It's the Full Moon. It brought out the real me in time to celebrate our new venture."

Mark nodded and held up his glass. "Here's to our future in Colorado and beyond."

He raised his glass with the others. He knew Mark had picked up on Danielle's swirling emotions and her new power. Something unlocked the well of magic inside her. No way he would have missed it from her photo. They had to take it slow, win her friendship and trust before asking her to be their mate. If they pushed too hard and fast, they could lose everything.

Unless the surge in her power meant she remembered who she is and is now ready to fulfill the prophecy. If that were the case, there would be no reason to hold back. She would know who they were and be drawn to them as well.

He decided to step back and let the Moon be their guide. It had been Mark's dreams that had sent them down this path and by all rights he should be the one to bond with Danielle first. Ian turned his attention toward reliving a fantasy from his past and indulging in a new one with Faye.

*

Mark's body vibrated until it aligned with the magical energy emanating from her. Every word she uttered spoke directly to his heart. His once restless Black Wolf quieted. In his mind, he pictured the creature curled up at her feet, eyes trained on her face. Eager to carry out her every wish.

She placed her hand over his. "I don't know how to explain it, but I feel like I've known you my whole life. You and Ian. How is that possible?"

"Anything's possible if you believe. I know that sounds corny—"

She shook her head and touched the moon on his forearm. "Not to me. Your tattoo changed."

"You can see it happen?" His heart beat faster. Every second dragged on in his head. The music from the band on stage faded to little more than white noise.

She leaned close until her lips were within an inch of his ear. Her warm breath kissed his skin as she answered. "Yes. Black Wolf. Ian's Gray, too."

"I heard my name over there. Don't believe a word he says about me, Dani."

"Lia filled me in on both of you." She smiled and licked her lips.

"And?" Ian draped his arm around Faye's shoulders.

Faye downed another shot. "She said the two of you could melt our panties off simply by walking in the room."

Mark grinned. "What's the verdict?"

Danielle poured another round for everyone and looked him dead in the eye. "I'm not wearing any."

All three men tossed back their shot. Faye raised hers up to toast her friend's sass and drank it down. Lia grabbed the bottle and chugged. "Nothing like a sexually charged conversation among friends with the same appetites."

He eased the bottle out of Lia's hands and filled their glasses again. Before their drinking went any further, he had to lay some ground rules. He knew Tony would never have included Faye in their party if she wasn't a friend of the magical world, but with the full moon rising, he had to be sure their wolves would be safe.

Ian smiled and nodded for him to go ahead. He nipped at Faye's ear. Her sexy giggle brought a smile to Danielle's face, too.

"Holy shit, Ian. Your tat changed to a wolf. How the hell did you do that?"

Tony cleared his throat to get her attention. "The three of us are shifters, chérie. We allow those we trust implicitly within our inner circle. The fact you can see the tattoo change is how you say...the cherry on top."

Lia winked. "You're officially one of us, momma."

"Does that mean I get to see all of ya'll naked?" She swept her hand around the table and smiled, not really expecting an answer to her naughty question. Her eyes sparkled reflecting the lights from the stage and over the bar and drew Ian in closer to her, almost hypnotizing him.

A disturbance at the front of the club prevented them from continuing with their conversation.

"Do you people think your boss is going to be happy with how you treat their clientele? I'll have you know, my wife knows them personally and if you value your jobs, you'll step aside and let us in."

An all too familiar nasal twang rang out over the music. "Danielle! Will you please call off your goons?"

The voice dragged out each syllable of her name, ensuring the maximum number of people would focus on her. All color drained from Danielle's face and she pursed her lips together.

Lia stood up and knocked her chair over in the process. "Mother fuckers have the nerve to show their faces here, tonight?"

"What the hell is that asshole, Sheldon, doing in Elko?" Ian's eyes narrowed and he emitted a low growl.

"The bitch with him is Dani's ex. I said if she showed up here I'd rip out her Walmart extensions. Hold these." She kicked off her heels and dropped them in Ian's lap.

Danielle held her hands up. "Stop. I can take care of this with a little back up. Mark and Ian, are you game?"

*

"What do you have in mind, darlin'?" Ian cracked his knuckles and downed another shot.

"I want to turn the tables and show her I've moved on. What better way to do that, then to put myself in the middle of the two of you?"

Mark smiled. "The one that got away. Perfect."

"We have history with Dylan from our days with SFPD. This is going to be fun."

She put her hand on Tony's shoulder as he stood to accompany them. "Let us handle this and take the heat off Taboo."

"We're not afraid of any heat or bad publicity, love. Family sticks together, but we'll do as you ask."

Faye and Lia agreed but didn't look thrilled about having to stay back. She couldn't love her soul sisters any more than she did at that moment.

She squared her shoulders and walked toward the entrance with Ian and Mark on either side of her. Her magic reached out and combined with theirs, forming an invisible shield around them. The crowd grew silent and parted to clear the path in front of her. She stopped a foot from the purple velvet rope. "The two of you are no longer welcome here. The rest of your party, however, is free to join in tonight's fun and entertainment."

"Come on, Dani. Everyone knows you're doing this out of spite. You're jealous I moved on to a life you've always wanted. Get over it."

Mark placed his hand on the small of her back. Ian closed in on her other side. She placed a palm on each of their cheeks. "You were saying?"

Amy's face turned crimson then deep purple. "Now you're into men? When did that happen?"

"Never stopped. You were a distraction. You have nothing I want now or ever."

"What the fuck, Amy? I thought we'd be able to stroll in here without any problems. You said you were awarded a part of this place in your settlement."

"Settlement? For what? Drunken booty calls a couple times a month? We were never married. Where do you get off thinking you're entitled to anything?"

Amy glared. "Nevada law sees it differently."

Danielle's laughter rang out. She leaned against Mark to keep upright as she tried to catch her breath. "Bitch, please. Without a marriage license, you get nada. *That* is according to Nevada law. We were barely roommates. Stop using Google for legal advice."

The crowd around them cheered. Those closest to them had their phones out recording the entire exchange. She suppressed a smile. Whatever Amy had hoped to achieve by creating a scene had blown up in her face.

Dylan tugged on his goatee. His eyes swept over her, lingering on her plunging neckline. "Damn, Dani. You've stepped up your game. Mmmmm. Looks like I chose the wrong broad to put the ring on. How about you let me in and we can talk about rectifying this situation?"

She felt the rumble in their chests against her back before she heard their growls. Dylan had always rubbed her the wrong way, but now he had crossed the line. "In your dreams, jackass."

Amy screamed and lunged. Her right arm swung out, her nails extended toward Danielle's face and neck. "Fucking bitch!"

Mark caught her by the wrist and twisted her arm behind her back. "Time for you to leave, or would you rather face attempted assault charges?"

Amy's battle cry turned to screaming insults and threats to sue everyone around them.

Dylan's eyes flew open. "Jesus H Christ! I thought I left the two of you pigs back in Cali."

Ian walked toward him, toe to toe forcing Dylan to back up until he hit the wall behind their friends. "Sucks to be you, Sheldon. You have one choice. Grab your wife and never set foot here again."

"Or what?"

"I tell everyone your real name. This time, your YouTube followers won't bail your ass out." Ian jerked his thumb toward the cameras recording every last detail.

Danielle snorted and turned toward the security detail. "I've had enough of this. If they're out of here within the next five minutes, I'm pressing charges."

She held out her hands to both men and smiled. "Come on. There's still a half bottle of tequila left to polish off and the party has yet to take off."

*

Ian pulled the two of them to the side. "If this is anything like we're going to experience in Colorado, I'm all in."

"Me, too." Mark grinned from ear to ear.

It had been some time since he had seen Mark enjoy himself like this. Their friends deserved a good deal of the credit for bringing Danielle into their world. Extra bonus came in the drop dead gorgeous creature that could very well match his sexual appetites.

Danielle nodded. "Before tonight, I wouldn't have been able to handle those two. I could feel your energy merging with mine. I felt on top of the world."

"As you should. You're a very powerful witch, Dani. You've barely begun to tap into it. We can help."

"Until tonight, part of my magic had been locked away. I saw you in a vision today as clear as the two of you standing in front of me now. We're supposed to be together, bonded…"

He and Mark spoke as one. "Mated."

She nodded. "I'm not gonna lie. I'm overwhelmed with all of this, but it feels right. *We* feel right."

"Whatever you need, however long it takes, we can figure it out together." He wasn't sure what else to say to reassure her she didn't have to rush into anything. They would wait until she was ready.

"Together. Speaking of that. I'd like to include everyone in a Full Moon ritual. Tonight, we're getting to know each other as a magical family. Tomorrow night, at the peak is when I would perform the official ceremony."

He looked to Mark for guidance. Whatever he wanted to do, he would do so without question. He tried to link their minds, but found the way blocked. That had never happened to them before, not since they were kids and learning how to use their powers.

"Have you ever been around wolves during the full moon? It can turn pretty damn intense in a blink of an eye. Not only with the shifting, but every emotion and desire will be amplified to a level higher than most humans can handle. Once the bonding starts, there's no turning back."

A stream of people filed past them in search of tables closer to the stage and bar. He tuned out their constant chatter and focused on his partners in front of him.

The intensity in her eyes matched that blazing in Mark's. "Have you ever been around a witch during a full moon?"

31

Ian shook his head and kept his mouth shut. He had an inkling where she intended to go with her questions.

"A Shaman. He was powerful, but you're better on the eyes."

He chuckled. "I agree."

A smile teased at the corners of her mouth but she kept her composure. "I perform my rituals in the nude and ask those with me to do the same. I bet your shaman didn't do that."

His body shuddered. "Don't tease an old man like that, darlin'."

The band launched into their cover of Joan Jett's "Do You Wanna Touch Me" and the crowd cheered, oblivious to the sparks flying between the three of them.

She licked her lips as she ran her fingertip down his abs to the top of his pants. She repeated the act with Mark. He wasn't sure what turned him on more, the fire she ignited over his skin with her touch or watching her bring his partner to his knees.

"*That* is a tease. The naked part is a promise."

Chapter 4

Mark warred with his Wolf for control. His howl echoed through his mind. He promised the beast Danielle would set him free to run wild that night and every night if he would keep under control for a little while longer.

She moved her palms to the center of each of their chests and closed her eyes. Within seconds, his racing heart slowed and his Wolf calmed. By the look on Ian's face, he had experienced the very same thing. Without a word, she tamed their beasts and allowed their minds to reconnect.

"Can you hear me?"

His eyes locked with Ian's. For their entire lives it had been the two of them. No one else had ever been able to speak to their minds at the same time. Not their pack leader. Not the shaman.

She tried to connect with them one more time. *"Please say something so I know I'm not imagining this."*

He placed his hand over hers. "Loud and clear."

"How?" Ian grasped her hand and held it tight against his heart.

She opened her eyes. "I don't know. I've been able to pick up bits and pieces since we met. That's why I must perform the ritual for this month's moon. I didn't realize how important it is for our future together until now."

He smiled. "This is our moon. If we would have arrived last month or were delayed until next..."

She gripped their hands. "The Wolf Moon calls out to us in a way no one outside our world could ever understand. I want to share that with Tony, Lia and Faye so that no matter where we are, we'll always find our way back to each other."

Ian grinned. "How about we join the others and resume the conversation. I believe Faye had posed a question to the group."

She held on to both of their hands as they wove their way through the evening bar and dinner crowd. The small intimacy sent jolts of fire through him. Every nerve ending came alive. Her voice, her scent, the contact with her soft skin all pulled him into her orbit. Everyone outside of their group faded away.

"You have the same effect on me, Mark."

He squeezed her fingers between his to signal he had heard every word. She turned to him and smiled. Her eyes promised him they would have their time together. For now, he planned to relax and follow her lead.

*

"I'm still miffed you wouldn't let us go up there with you, but damn, Boo! YouTube blew *up* with it! I thought Dylan was gonna piss his pants." Faye tapped the video on her phone to rewind and view the scene again. She threw back her head and let loose with the laughter that made your cheeks hurt from smiling and your lungs scream from lack of air.

Ian handed her one of the linen napkins from the table to dab the tears at the corners of her eyes. "It wouldn't be the first time he'd soiled himself in front of us."

"I can believe it. So, what were the three of you talking about after they hauled off the troublemakers?"

Mark grabbed the bottle of tequila and checked the level. "We're going to need another. This one is running on fumes."

She signaled to the bartender to send over another and returned her hand to rest in Mark's lap. He turned in his seat so her back rested against his chest. In this position, he had easy access to her neck and bare shoulder. The idea his lips could be on her skin in an instant, wound her body tighter and tighter.

She rested her head against his shoulder and winked toward Faye. "Ian reminded me we never answered your question."

"You're going to have to be a bit more specific. As you can see by the bottle, we've had a couple rounds watching your performance at the door." She reached for her empty glass and flipped it over.

Ian turned her glass back and filled it with the last of the previous bottle of tequila. "I can't speak for everyone else, but I intend to see every part of you naked tonight. It's only fair I return the favor."

"She's already seen me naked."

Lia filled the rest of the glasses from the new bottle of Patron. "Me, too."

Tony appeared genuinely disappointed and held his hand over his heart as if he had been stabbed. "I'm feeling left out of all this nakedness. How did I not get the memo to see all three of you in the buff?"

Faye turned her attention toward her. "I take it we'll all be stripping in the moonlight?"

She nodded. "How does three nights grab you?"

Mark wrapped his arm around her and traced his fingertips up and down her ribcage. "I'm game."

Faye's eyes locked with hers. "You know how I feel about you. Please don't tease me with that."

Danielle stood up and walked around the table. She took Faye's face in her hands and kissed her the way she should have done years ago. "You are my heart and soul sister."

Faye seemed to be overcome with emotion and unable to speak, but her eyes told Danielle she was ready to hear her out.

"This could be the last time we're all together here. It's my job to create fantasies for other people. Let me help do the same for you."

Tony reached for Faye's hand. "What do you say, mon chérie? It's been a long time coming, no?"

She knew Faye wanted to give in, but her old fears held her back. Far too many nights she had spent alone instead of facing the humiliation of another man calling her a freak. Somehow, she had to find a way to reassure Faye she had nothing to worry about in their group.

"I got this, darlin'"

She kissed Faye again and returned to her place next to Mark.

Ian took Faye's free hand into his. "What's holding you back from having all your hidden desires fulfilled?"

She sighed. "You and Mark need to know something about me before we go any further."

Ian kissed her. "Sweetheart, the only thing that matters is here and now. Past is past."

Faye shook her head. "Pour another round Lia my love. Maybe two."

Mark pulled her a little closer, sensing her concern for Faye. She focused their combined magic and sent it out toward her friend.

"I was a regular here at Taboo in the early days, back when outsiders felt the need to come here to tell Elko how to handle the influx of the kinksters and homos. That's what they called us then and I was one of their favorite targets."

Mark inhaled sharply. "Before you transitioned?"

Faye's eyes widened. "How did you guess that?"

He smiled and Danielle sensed the compassion pouring out of him. "Shifters come in all shapes, sizes and sexual orientation. We recognize kindred spirits immediately, even if they're not part of the magical world."

He pointed to his heart. "You are one of us in here. Surgery helped with the outside so it matched your spirit."

Ian brought her hand to his lips. "Is that what you were worried about?"

Faye nodded. "I was born David Hernandez."

Ian placed his hand over her heart. "Have you always been Faye Ellis in here?"

"Yes." Tears welled up in her eyes.

"In your mind?" His thumb brushed against her temple.

"Yes." Her voice came out as a hoarse whisper.

"In your soul?"

No one spoke. All held their breath waiting for her answer.

"Always and forever."

"That's all that matters to me."

Tony patted her hand in his. "Has been for all of us, chérie. We've been waiting for you to be ready."

Faye's jaw dropped. "You knew?"

"That you've been in love with me all along? Oui."

Faye tossed back her drink. "This is supposed to be your night, Boo. What's happening?"

Lia cleared her throat. "I got this one. The Wolf Moon is what's happening. It brought all of us here, to this place for a reason. Sex is powerful magic and it can unite all of our worlds."

"Are you sure? I don't want to ruin what we have now."

Lia reached for Tony's hand. We want this with you and have for some time. Ian is the cherry on top."

"You okay with this?" Mark whispered in her ear. His breath on her neck sent her stomach fluttering out of control.

She nodded. "I'm still getting used to the idea we're meant to be a threesome. I thought I'd ease into it with the two of us tonight. Is that okay with you?"

"Not a doubt in my mind but we might want to move our party to your rooms. The moon is rising and I believe we promised Faye stripping in the moonlight?"

"Taboo is known for it's wild parties. Our clientele wouldn't bat an eye if we did it on the center stage with the band playing on around us."

He nuzzled her bare neck and planted a kiss in the middle of one of her hot zones. The rush of heat between her legs caused her to clamp her thighs together and lean into him.

"I don't share my lovers with anyone other than Ian and the group at this table. Everyone else can go fuck themselves."

She shuddered as the last words left his lips. In that instant, she wasn't sure they would make it out of the elevator before he had her pinned against the wall screaming his name. She willed herself to focus.

Ian smiled and lifted his chin. "You two go on up. We have a few more things to discuss. Don't we darlin'?"

Faye blushed. "That we do."

Her heart swelled with love. She had never seen her bestie so happy.

Mark stood and held his hand out to her. "She's in good hands. Now it's your turn. I have this image burned into my brain from a sexy witch in an elevator."

"You saw that? Fuck. Me."

"Yes, I did and that would be the plan."

He led her through the throng of people around the bar toward the bank of elevators near the entrance of the club. Any one of them would take them to her floor, but she refused to wait with the other guests.

She dug her heels in and tugged on his hand. "Hold up."

He pulled her into his arms and planted kisses along her neck. "Having second thoughts?"

"You might want to use this." Her fingers dipped into a hidden pocket in the strap of her halter and removed a special keycard for the private elevator at the end of the hallway.

His pupils dilated as his fingers covered hers. "You take your elevator fantasies seriously, don't you?"

She moved out of his arms and nodded. "I've been patient long enough. As soon as those doors close behind us, you're all mine."

Mark's eyes locked with hers. She backed up step-by-step. He matched her move for move but kept mere inches between them. She bit her lip as he inserted the keycard into the slot to activate the panel. The doors opened and he closed the gap between them, lifting her up in his arms. His lips crushed hers.

Danielle wrapped her legs around his waist and ground her pelvis against him. Her tongue slipped and slid over his, taking control then yielding. His scent, his taste and his heat overwhelmed her senses and she lost all control.

He held her up against the wall in the corner of the elevator, his hands slid over her ass. He dug his fingers into her flesh as their kiss deepened.

The soft chime announcing they had arrived on her floor to her penthouse suite broke the spell between them. She clung to him. Both of them panting.

"First door on the right," she whispered against his throat.

Mark growled. "Now."

He reached between them and freed his cock. He slid the head between her slick folds.

She whimpered and braced herself. All thoughts of getting safely into the suite evaporated as he entered her. He spread her legs wider, buried his cock deep in her pussy and groaned.

"Mark. Mark. Mark." She called his name with each thrust into her. She clung to him as he drove them faster and faster. Her pussy spasmed around his pulsing cock. Her body quaked as the fire between them raged out of control.

His muscles rippled and jumped against her fingertips as she explored everything within her reach.

She screamed as another orgasm tore through her. She opened her eyes to find two glowing orbs staring back at her.

He tipped his head back and howled.

"Mine. Mine. Mine."

The Black Wolf joined with him to claim their mate. First her body and then her spirit yielded to them, giving herself over completely to their insatiable lust and desire.

They took her over and over again until all three exploded together.

The air around them crackled with ancient magic released from the spell that had kept them apart from the White Witch for centuries.

*

"Mark? Come back, lover."

He shook his head to clear the fog from his mind. He still held her up against the back of the elevator. His cock pulsing and emptying his seed deep inside her. He silently cursed himself for taking her like that, without protection.

She wiped the sweat from his forehead. Her voice trembled. Not with fear, but from aftershocks of her last climax. "You okay?"

He nodded and raised his eyebrows. "We weren't alone?"

She smiled. "Does that happen every time you have sex?"

He lifted her away from the wall and carried her out of the elevator. He knew he should let her go, but he was afraid if he did, all of it would disappear.

Like every other time in his dreams.

She kissed his eyelids, both cheeks and then his lips. "This isn't a dream."

He eased out of her eliciting a soft gasp from her. "Are you hurt?"

She shook her head. "No. Like you, I wanted to stay connected for as long as possible. Plus, I wasn't sure your wolf would've allowed it to happen."

He leaned against the wall as she slid the keycard in the door. Her skin glistened with a fine sheen of sweat and the blush over her cheeks traveled down her neck to her breasts. He licked his lips at the image of her stretched out naked next to him in the moonlight.

She took his hand and walked through the doorway and into the living room. The view through the floor to ceiling window wall in front of him took his breath away and added more to the images playing out in his mind. The silhouettes of the mountains called out to him and to his wolf. This would be what they would see out of their windows once they moved home to Colorado.

Home with her.

"You didn't answer my question. Has Black Wolf ever come out and joined with you like that?"

"Only with you. I'm betting it's going to happen when you join with Ian, too."

She smoothed the front of his shirt and rested her cheek against his chest. "I wasn't afraid when he came out, Mark. I can't explain it, but I knew he wouldn't hurt me."

He rubbed her back and shoulders. He wished he could say without a doubt Black Wolf wouldn't ever harm her. He and Ian had never experienced anything like this before. "We're all flying by the seat of our pants with this. Shaman and your Crone have provided us with enough guidance to find each other. With your magic returning and growing, we'll learn as we go and more will be revealed to us."

She turned her face up to look in his eyes. "The moon is near its peak. Taboo owns the acreage from the resort to Elko Mountain. If you and Ian need to run free, you'll be safe."

He kissed her forehead. "The view from your windows did call out to me, but Black Wolf is calm and at peace thanks to you. We'll break out tomorrow night before the ceremony."

"In that case, what do you say we christen the hot tub and then order some food?"

He placed his hand over his heart. "You're speaking my language now. Hot tub involves getting naked with you and I seem to have worked up an incredible appetite."

She grinned. "For me or the food?"

He nuzzled her neck. "Both."

"How about a tour before we dive back into each other? I wouldn't want you to get lost in the middle of the night on your way back to bed from the bathroom. You may think that's an odd thing to think of but having been in that exact situation before, I make it a point to know my surroundings."

"You're adorable."

He held her hand as she opened the sliding glass doors from the living room out to the balcony. Six floors up from the ground floor provided enough privacy to be able to wander about the suite naked without having to obscure the mountain view. The deck balcony continued the length of the suite and could be accessed from the bedroom as well. "Of course, if we have a busy night and need more shut eye, we can tint the windows to block out the light."

He tossed the remote she handed him onto the wrap around sofa. "Is that the champagne Ian and I sent over earlier?" He pointed to the bar area near the entryway.

She blushed. "Faye and I polished it off. I needed a little liquid courage to meet you. Since she cut my hair this afternoon, my brain has been running on fast-forward through visions, memories and dreams. I wanted to focus."

He rubbed his thumb over her cheek. "Why do you think we started the shots before you joined us? Ian and I have been in knots too."

"Good to know." She winked and led him toward the kitchen.

"I like the semi-open floor plan you have in here and in Tony's suite. The vaulted ceilings make both places look huge."

"That's the idea. We don't have the towers that the big cities have but we wanted to provide the same illusion. There are six other suites like this one and they are booked out two years in advance now."

The kitchen was twice the size of the efficiency they had in California and decorated with a modern flare, with splashes of the pinks, purples and blacks of Taboo's signature décor. As they moved down the hallway, artwork and personal photos decorated the off-white painted walls. Each item provided him a small glimpse into her world, all of it centered on Tony, Lia and Faye. No other people adorned her walls. He filed the information away to ask her later.

"This is where I spend my down time, not that I have much of it." The California King centered against the wall farthest from the door way appeared warm and inviting. Covered in pillows of various sizes and shades of purple and a down filled comforter the bed promised hours of comfort and sleep.

Tonight, sleep was the last thing on his mind.

She crooked her finger and beckoned him to follow her to the master bath connected to her bedroom. A large sunken tub took up one corner of the room. By the size of it, he figured it would hold at least four people. The black granite tub matched the stone sinks. All had silver faucets and accents. Thick fluffy towels hung on warming racks and deep mauve and purple rugs had been strategically placed over the marble flooring. His eyes took it all in and conjured up another fantasy of the three of them in the tub.

She turned the silver faucet handles until satisfied with the temperature. She stood and smiled. "It will take a few minutes to fill. Follow me."

As she walked away from him, her hands slid down her hips to the hem of her dress. She grasped the material between her fingers and dragged it up her body.

He held his breath. Mesmerized by her every move. Inch by inch she revealed more of her curves. His mouth watered and his desire for her soared. The ache to have her again teetered on the edge of pain.

She stopped at the foot of her bed and turned toward him again. In one smooth, fluid motion she freed herself of the dress and tossed it to him. She stood before him in nothing but her thigh high boots. "Care to give me a hand with these?"

He drank in every inch of her as he approached and knelt at her feet. His hand cupped her calf and raised it to rest on his shoulder as he unzipped the form fitting suede. He repeated the process with the other boot.

"I've never seen anyone look more beautiful."

"You make me believe it."

His heart broke with those words. The pain in her voice pierced his soul. He reached out to her mind, unable to verbalize the question.

"I don't understand. Why have you thought otherwise?"

*

She meant it. Others have leered and lusted after her, but never like this. It was in the way he touched her back to give her strength when confronting Amy. The way he curved his body to fit with hers when they sat at the table with the others. It was in the way he both dominated and submitted to her.

"I see myself through your eyes. It's as if I've been locked away in a dark place. You set me free."

He scooped her off the bed and up into his arms. He rested his forehead against hers. "No one will ever confine you again."

"You and Ian walk into my life right when I needed you the most. I had thought I was going to live the rest of my life with a huge part of me missing."

Mark sat down on the dressing table bench and kept her on his lap. "I've dreamed of you for so long, I had started to think you didn't exist. That all changed the instant Lia showed us a picture of you on her phone. My one regret is that it took so long for us to take Tony up on his invitation."

Her lips brushed over his. "Shh. No regrets. Time to get you naked."

His palm caressed her cheek. "As you wish."

She stood and helped him remove his clothes. She kissed and licked her way down his chest with each button until his shirt fell away from his body. She rubbed his dick through his pants and her pussy throbbed with the memory of the pleasure it brought to her over and over again. She opened his fly and shoved his pants down over his hips.

He moaned and sighed as her fingers encircled his shaft. Her tongue swirled round and round the head. "Dani…"

She stepped away from him long enough to turn off the water. She held out her hand to him. "Want to help me check off another fantasy from my bucket list?"

He gripped her fingers as she eased down into the steaming water and then sat across from her. He brought her feet into his lap and massaged her arches. "You've never had sex in a hot tub?"

Danielle shrugged. "Hadn't met anyone I wanted to share the experience with until now."

He separated her ankles and floated her from her seat into his lap. He crushed her tits against his chest. He lifted her up enough to slip his cock into her

"Is this what you had in mind?" He captured her lower lip and pinched it between his teeth.

"It's as if you can read my thoughts." She winked and pulled his head back to get access to his neck. She snaked her tongue along his stubbly chin, savoring the sweet and saltiness.

He balanced her body with his hands on her hips, holding her in place.

She arched her back as he eased her body down the rest of the way. She rocked her hips forward and back, sliding along his shaft and stimulating every nerve ending in her G-spot.

He flicked her right nipple with the tip of his tongue until it puckered and stood at attention. His mouth sealed over it and he sucked hard.

Her fingers tangled in his hair as she held him in place. "Yes, baby. Harder. Suck. Harder."

He squeezed both of her breasts together, popped her nipple out of his mouth and latched onto the other.

Danielle's body convulsed and her mind exploded with images of wolves running through mountains on fire in search of a fallen angel, witches and the Fae on the brink of war. Pleasure and pain forever entwined.

"Come back, sweetheart."

She opened her eyes to find herself still in the hot tub and in Mark's arms. "What happened?"

He chuckled. "You fucked me silly and then blacked out."

"But I saw—"

"I know. We're still connected with Ian too. There will be time enough to sort through your vision tomorrow."

She smiled and turned to rest her back against his chest. The warm water swirled around them and helped to ease the tension she hadn't realized she had been carrying around with her all day. She tilted her head back to rest against his shoulder; her forehead nestled under his chin. "I've had spotty visions here and there all my life. This is the first time they've come so fast and clear. They're not riddles but flashes of the future in Ouray."

He reached for the scrunchy and loaded it with her favorite body wash. "Between the six of us, we'll be able to piece it all together. Will you let me take care of you now?"

"I'm not used to being pampered."

His soapy hands caressed her skin. "Good time to start. This time tomorrow night, you'll have two of us spoiling you."

She turned to face him. "There won't be any problems between you and Ian? I know the two of you have been with Tony and Lia, but this is different."

Mark shook head. "Honey, you have nothing to worry about on that front. Until we found you, I had been worried Ian and I would have to separate to find out mates. He hadn't told me about his dreams of you until this afternoon. He wanted the two of us to bond first."

Danielle rubbed the soapy scrunchy over his shoulders and his back. "You're amazing."

His mouth turned up at one corner and his eyes dazzled from the reflection of the soft overhead lighting. "This is the start of our life together. We have a lot to learn and explore. It's exciting and a tad daunting. That's as it should be."

"There is so much I don't understand, so much I want to ask both of you. It's as if I've been in a fog my whole life and it's finally lifted. Now I can see, but what does it all mean?"

Chapter 5

Ian braced his forearms on top of the deck railing and closed his eyes. He inhaled the crisp desert air. The faint pine scent from Elko Mountain in the distance brought back memories of running through the Siskiyou Range in northern California. He had longed for that kind of freedom again and here he was about to have his wish granted. His body hummed with the intensity of the orgasm he shared with Mark and Danielle through their psychic connection. The night breeze danced over his bare skin but did very little to cool the fire coursing through his veins.

Gray Wolf rested, knowing his time would come to be with their mate. Faye and Lia had both managed to calm the beast and quenched Ian's thirst for excitement. However, his mind pulled him back to Danielle's visions of Ouray.

The soft whisper of the sliding glass door behind him brought him out of his thoughts. Lia's hands slid over his shoulders. "I thought I might find you out here."

He wrapped his arm around her. "You should be in bed."

She kissed him and dug her fingers into his bare ass. "You should be with Dani and Mark. Don't get me wrong, lover. You fulfilled more than a few fantasies of mine tonight and I can say with all confidence you rocked Faye's universe."

He laughed and hugged her close. "So why are you trying to kick me out?"

"Your heart belongs to our best friends. I didn't believe it until I saw the three of you together. I've not witnessed that sort of connection since the day you introduced me to my Bear. Besides, once Faye and Tony seal their bond tonight, he's not going to want to share her again with you any time soon."

Faye's sighs and moans reached his ears. Choosing to have sex with her had been a no brainer as far as he was concerned. Her body had brought him great pleasure and he had been honored to do the same for her. The thought that anyone would treat her as anything but the glorious goddess she was pissed him off to no end. The idea that Tony and Lia would bring her into their lives and bed made perfect sense. The love between them had been obvious from the start. Being a part of that had been an extra bonus for him.

"I've missed you, darlin'. You always could read me better than anyone, even Mark."

"You and I have a special connection. Our souls are wild and need to be free to experience all that life offers. We've been blessed with soul mates who allow us to be ourselves without judgement."

He thanked the Wolf Moon for bringing all of them together here and now. Everything is as it should be and he wasn't about to question any of it.

"She was able to connect with our minds and with a touch of her hand she calmed our wolves. No one has been able to do that before."

"There you go. What the hell are you waiting for? Complete your bond now. It will make the ceremony tomorrow night all the more powerful. You'll need it for Ouray. There's something big brewing. I can't quite put my finger on it."

The chorus of "Hungry Like the Wolf" rang out from his phone in the living room."

Lia raised an eyebrow. "Duran Duran? Seriously?"

He laughed. "What do you want me to use as his ringtone? Who's Afraid of the Big Bad Wolf?"

She wrapped her arms around his neck and kissed him, like she did the night they first met. "Go on before I change my mind and keep you for myself."

He snatched the phone from the mahogany coffee table. "Is everything okay?"

Lia smiled and blew him another kiss. She sashayed down the candlelit hall and back into the bedroom. He smiled as his eyes zeroed in on his clothes, neatly folded and draped over the end of the couch.

"Better than okay. Can you break away now? Dani suggested the three of us have a late dinner here in the suite."

"Perfect timing. I'm starving and we have a hell of a lot to talk about. Give me twenty minutes and I'll grab our gear from the room."

"No need. Dani had everything moved an hour ago. All we need now is you."

"On my way." He stepped into his jeans and slid his arms into his shirt. He sat down to put on his socks and shoes as Faye stepped through the double doors of the bedroom.

She leaned her shoulder against the wall causing the top of her robe to fall down her opposite arm. Her hair cascaded down her back in a wild mass of curls. His mouth watered at the sight of her. "Were you going to leave without saying goodbye?"

"Not on your life, beautiful. Didn't want to pull you away from the bear too soon." He crossed the distance between them as she stood up from the wall. He held her face in his hands as his mouth devoured hers.

She clung to him and yielded completely. She smiled as he ended the kiss. "Lia wasn't kidding."

"About the melting panties thing?"

She nodded. Her eyes glistened. "Thank you for making me feel beautiful inside and out."

"Because you are and always have been."

Faye finished buttoning his shirt for him. The wood in the fireplace snapped and crackled as the flames slowly turned the logs into coals. "Enough of this mushy stuff. You don't want to keep Boo waiting if you know what's good for ya."

He kissed the tip of her nose. "I hear that. Go on back to bed. Tony will be wondering what's taking you so long. We'll catch up tomorrow."

Ian showed himself out of the suite and sprinted through the empty corridors until he reached Danielle's rooms. He filled his lungs and exhaled to a count of ten in an attempt to slow his racing heart. He reached out to rap his knuckles on the door as it swung open.

She stood there in a purple silk kimono that barely brushed the top of her thighs. Her scent overwhelmed him and he had to brace his hands on the doorframe to keep his knees from buckling. Gray Wolf leapt to attention and panted.

"Mine. Mine. Mine."

*

Goosebumps peppered her skin. Ian's eyes transitioned from dark brown to gold and back again. The veins in his forearms bulged. She opened her arms to him and he appeared to struggle with accepting her invitation.

She met him at the door and wrapped her arms around his waist. "Look at me, Ian. Please."

His eyes locked with hers. "I can't hold him back any longer. Not this close to you."

"No one is asking you to."

"Mark…"

She backed away and dropped her robe to the floor. "He'll be back with the food in a bit. This was his idea."

His eyes never left hers as he followed her inside and closed the door. She backed up until she reached the couch. He angled his chin to the right and then the left and closed his eyes. "I've pictured this moment with you so many times."

His whispered confession spoke directly to her heart. She understood why he had held back from telling Mark about his dreams. They had been searching for her all this time and both had been afraid to trust their dreams were real. She had done the same thing.

"Don't think. Live the moment."

She stretched out on the blanket she had placed over the cushions. Her naked body glistened in moonlight pouring in from the windows. She presented herself as a gift from the Moon Goddess, one he had prayed for every night for as far back as he could remember. He popped every button from his shirt as he tore it from his body. She unfastened his jeans and shoved them down over his hips, freeing his cock. Her fingers wrapped around the shaft. He gasped as she stroked his length, up and over the velvety tip.

His lips brushed over hers as the tips of their tongues swirled around each other. He tasted of tequila and sex. Sweet and salty. Exciting and familiar all at the same time.

He hooked the back of her knees over his arms and spread her legs wide as he drove his cock inside her pussy. She arched her back and surrendered to the fire raging between them. His muscles strained and pulsed against her fingertips. Raw power surged through their bodies triggering a wave of desire within her so strong it threatened to consume them both. She called out to his wolf, ready to complete their mating bond.

"Come to me now, Gray Wolf."

The beast leapt at her command and joined with Ian. The deep rumbling in his chest grew louder and louder with each orgasm that slammed through her body. An explosion of color filled her mind as images of rings of fire around a mountain battlefield come into view. Fairy against fairy. Witch against witch.

She came to, clinging to Ian, and both of them gasping.

He rolled them onto their sides and brushed her hair from her face. "We won't let anything hurt you again, Dani."

"You saw the battlefield?"

"And everything from before with Mark."

She retrieved her robe and his jeans from the floor and returned to sit with him. "Both of your wolves have called me the White Witch. I never thought I was the one the prophecy foretold. She's supposed to be of both lines of fairy blood, Seelie and Unseelie."

"You are. Mark and I were able to pick it up from your picture."

Danielle went over everything her grandparents had told her about her family and not once had they mentioned the double lineage. "My grandmother told me my father was a prince of the Unseelie Court. She said it was an embarrassment to our family and she refused to talk about him any further. I don't remember my mother or anything about her being from the Seelie Court."

He held her hand. "We'll figure it out. Together."

They turned toward the entryway at the sound of the door opening. Mark's smiling face peeked around the edge. "Everyone decent?"

"Barely, but you already knew that." She grinned and got up to help him bring the serving cart through the door. The aroma from the covered dishes was enough to set off a symphony in her stomach. He had managed to bring all of her favorites. She wasn't surprised considering their connection.

Mark removed the covers from the plates revealing steak and twice baked potatoes along with a heaping of grilled vegetables. "Your chef assured me you haven't had steak in quite some time."

Ian rubbed his hands together. "Porterhouse rare. Perfect."

They sat around her dining room table savoring every bite and learning more about each other. With their bond, she probably could search their minds for the information she wanted, but instead chose the old-fashioned way. She had not been surprised to learn their friendship had started when they were kids. While they each had other relationships, Ian and Mark had always found their way back to each other, as friends and lovers. She had been more of a loner as a child and treated as an outcast. It wasn't until she met Tony and Lia that she felt acceptance.

"When did you find out you were shifters?"

Ian sipped his beer and appeared to mull over her question. "I was thirteen or fourteen when I first changed but Gray Wolf spoke to me my whole life. It freaked me out enough to seek out help from the local medicine man."

"I was fascinated with everything Native American and spent all my free time on the reservation listening to the old stories from the Elders. My parents encouraged me to seek out Shaman. That's where I met Ian for the first time."

"He followed me around like a lost puppy dog."

Mark laughed. "Don't let him fool you. He loved having a little brother to boss around."

"I remember very little of my childhood before I was sent to live with my grandparents. I didn't have anyone to talk to about magic until I was sent to spend a summer with an elderly witch my grandmother referred to as The Crone."

Ian refilled their water glasses and continued their conversation. "How old were you when that happened?"

His innocent question set unlocked a flood of memories. She gripped the table as each one flew by at high speed. She saw herself walking through trails high in the mountains collecting plants and herbs hand in hand with Nanny Rowan and her sisters. All four of Fairy blood. Their names flashed in front of her eyes as each witch's face came into view.

Fiona, Jessalyn, Rowan and…

Her grandmother, Eileen.

*

He knelt on the floor at her feet while Ian ran to the kitchen for a cold compress for her neck. "Who were those women, Dani?"

Her body shook and she gripped his fingers. "Mm…my grandmother Eileen and her sisters. All this time. She knew all this time and she kept it from me."

Ian draped the washcloth over the back of her neck and joined him on the floor next to her chair. "Fiona is who you know of as the Crone, isn't she?"

Danielle nodded. "I thought she was my one connection to magic. Apparently, she's much more than that."

He kissed her hand and held it to his cheek. "Do you recognize where you were?"

"In the mountains near Ouray."

"Remember, dear heart. Remember where you came from. It's time you come home with your wolves. Ouray needs the White Witch and her Guardians."

Ian's eyes widened. "Who was that?"

"Nanny Rowan. She's been calling to me since the two of you arrived in town."

He stood and helped her from the chair. "Is there a way we can contact her, maybe meet with her and the other sisters after we move in?"

"I hope so. We sure as hell won't get any answers from my grandmother, if that is who she really is."

"What do you mean, darlin'?" Ian joined them on the couch and took her other hand.

"The earliest memories I have of unconditional love come from Nanny Rowan and Jessalyn. Not once have I felt anything like that with Eileen or her husband. They took me in out of a sense of family duty, not because they wanted a connection with my mother."

Mark's heart went out to her. He didn't know how anyone could handle all the information and raw emotion she had to experience in less than a day. He wrapped one of the throw blankets from the sofa around her shoulders to help slow her trembling.

Ian's eyes locked with his. Now that they had found her, both of them looked forward to a night of peaceful slumber. "We're not going to find any more answers tonight. My vote is to curl up in that California King and give our brains a rest."

She kissed him and then Ian. "Falling asleep between the two of you is going to be rough, but I think I can manage it."

Ian kissed her again. "You two go on ahead. I'll take care of the dinner mess and hit the shower."

Danielle wobbled as she shuffled toward the bedroom. He scooped her up into his arms and carried her the rest of the way. "Too much excitement, good food and tequila for me. Good idea calling it a night."

He sat her on the end of the bed and turned down the covers. "I have to warn you. Both of us have been known to snore."

She giggled and dropped her robe to the floor. She slipped between the silk sheets and patted the spot next to her. "Me, too."

Mark stripped out of his clothing and joined her. She nestled close to his body, her head resting on his left shoulder. She turned on her side and lifted her head. "Wait. Do you prefer the right or left side of the bed?"

"Your eyes are drooping and you're worried about that?"

She smiled and pinched his nipple. "I want optimal snuggling and spooning, Mister Man. If either one of you isn't comfortable, it won't work."

He pulled her back to his body propped up on the pillows. "This is perfect."

Ian strode through the door on his way to the master bathroom. "As long as you're in the middle, I'm not complaining. Hold up. Are you moon tats glowing?"

*

Danielle glanced at her left hip and gasped. In the center of the Celtic Knot the head of a brown and gray wolf had formed. She flipped over to examine her right hip. Sure enough, a black wolf head had appeared. His eyes staring straight into hers.

Mark's fingers circled the new ink. "This wasn't here when we were in the hot tub."

"The other is new, too. You didn't feel them change?" Ian approached the bed to inspect her skin more closely.

She shook her head. "Not even a tingling sensation. Faye had touched one of the moons when we were getting dressed and it zapped her. Her fingers were burned where they touched my skin and then they were normal as if nothing happened."

Ian reached out with his right hand to touch her skin and froze. "Let me see your tat, Mark."

They held out their arms side by side. Below each wolf a new symbol emerged, incorporated within the neck hair. A gold Celtic Knot entwined with a blood red heart appeared to pulse in front of their eyes, matching the heartbeat of their wolves.

Danielle smiled. "Soul mates. The Crone…Fiona told me The White Witch and her Guardians had been marked so they would be able to find each other in every lifetime. This proves we are the three to fulfill the prophecy. My mother had to be of Seelie bloodline."

"Okay, my brain has officially overloaded. Shower then sleep." Ian tossed his jeans on the floor next to her robe. As he walked out of the room, she noted the tattoos covering his well-muscled back and thighs, similar to the ink covering Mark's body.

She got up and stood in front of the full-length mirror in her closet. The moons on her hips had indeed changed to a different color and appeared larger, more like that of a super moon. She caught Mark's reflection in the mirror. He propped his head on his hand as he watched her.

"Come back to bed ma chérie, Danielle."

"As you wish."

The hardwood floor felt cool against the souls of her feet. Up until that point, she hadn't noticed the drop in the room temperature. She shivered and dove under the covers. She pressed her body against Mark's warm skin. Every muscle in her body relaxed as she listened to the steady rhythm of his heart beating in his chest. She draped her arm over his abdomen and hugged him close.

As her mind floated toward sleep, Ian spooned his body with hers; his cock nestled between her thighs. His arm rested under hers, completing their circle. The last thing she remembered was the sound of Rowan's voice.

"Sleep well my precious child. We will be here waiting for you and your wolves."

Chapter 6

"Rise and shine, Boo."

She opened one eye to find Faye's head on the pillow next to her. She smiled and reached for her friend. "I guess I don't have to ask you how last night went with Tony and Lia. The smile on your face and the glow in your cheeks says it all."

Faye kissed her. "I can say the same about you. I came over to pick up my stuff and found the three of you sound asleep in the center of the bed. I don't think I've ever seen you look so peaceful."

Danielle thought back and had to admit her friend was right. Not only had she been able to sleep without any crazy jumbled dreams, her body felt refreshed and full of energy. Good thing too since they had a full day ahead along with preparing for the ritual. "I feel fucking fantastic."

"The feeling is unanimous. Right now, your men are in the kitchen. I'm supposed to distract you long enough for them to serve you breakfast in bed. You better make your bathroom run now so I can say I fulfilled my promise."

"Good call." She tossed back the covers and bolted for the bathroom. She laughed at the thought she'd lasted this long without having to untangle herself from Mark and Ian in order to pee. On the back of the door, someone had hung up her big fluffy bathrobe, still warm from the dryer. In the pockets she found a pair of socks with nonslip bottoms that Faye had given to her for Christmas.

She wrapped the robe around her body, brushed her teeth and fluffed up her spikey hair. She glanced into the open dopp kits on the vanity. Their choice of toothpaste and mouthwash mimicked her own which would make for a less cluttered vanity after the move to their new home. She noted the brands of deodorant, shampoos and body wash. She had learned the best way to get to know a person is to snoop around in their medicine cabinet or toiletry bags.

She picked up the aftershave from both of them and inhaled. Each scent similar but different enough to tell which belonged to each man. Her body flushed from head to toe reliving every moment, every touch and kiss. Tonight, the three of them would go all in and pledge themselves to each other under the Wolf Moon. Their transformation would be complete.

She opened the door, popped her head out and looked to see if she was still in the clear. "Faye?"

"Get your ass back here!"

The hoarse whisper lit a fire under her ass and shot her adrenaline into overdrive. She squealed and dove over Faye's body and back under the covers. Their laughter rang out as the men walked in with bed trays loaded with food, coffee and a pot of her favorite tea.

Mark and Ian joined them, sitting on either side, mugs of coffee in hand. She sipped her tea and listened to Faye tell them all about her night.

Ian nicked a piece of Faye's bacon and barely missed having a fork stabbed in his fingers. He laughed and kissed her neck. "Apparently Tony has big plans for you today. Care to share?"

Faye blushed and sipped her coffee. "They've asked me to move in and make it all official."

She squeezed Faye's thigh under the covers. "Look at you. I told you love would find you when you weren't looking."

"Or when magical worlds collide." Mark draped his arm around her shoulders and nibbled on her ear lobe.

She smiled and leaned back against him. "Taboo II has been open since Christmas for special groups and VIP invitations to try out the resort and provide us with their honest feedback."

"A soft opening?" Ian settled back against the pillows and drank the rest of his coffee.

"Exactly. So far, we've had rave reviews and the reservations for the grand opening party have flooded in. Based on the response, Jensen and Carter have recommended we spread the party out over a three-day weekend."

She brought them up to date on the resort and the struggles they have had with some of the town council members. "Two years ago, there had been a petition presented to the council calling for them to revoke our permit for the resort. The mayor had gone to bat for us and continues to be one of Taboo's biggest allies. His family owns the Tailwind resort south of Ouray proper."

Faye tapped one of her nails on her tray. "Oh! I've heard of that place. One of my clients got married there last spring. Lucky for them they moved their wedding up. Their original date put them right smack dab in the middle of wildfire season."

"Overall, Ouray is a welcoming community and they take care of their own and the surrounding communities. Especially during fire season." She grabbed the remote from one of the cubbies in above their heads. She punched in a series of numbers and the cabinet in front of them opened to reveal a large flat screen.

"I asked Jensen to interview some of the locals about their hometown so we could get a feel for it through their eyes. I thought if we watched it together now, it might trigger more or at the very least bring clarity to what I've been shown so far."

She brought the video files on the smart TV. She pushed the microphone button and waited for the tone. "Play Mayor's Welcome."

Lester Ross smiled and waved into the camera. He tipped his cowboy hat up to reveal more of his weather worn features. "Hello. I'm Lester Ross, Mayor of the Switzerland of America. Most folks think Ouray got that nickname because of where we're located in the middle of the mountains. In actuality, our town and the surrounding area is the epicenter for all the magic in this universe."

Mark's jaw dropped. "He did *not* just say that."

Ian snorted. "Like hell he didn't."

Faye slapped Ian's thigh. "Shush. I want to hear what he says."

Danielle focused every fiber of her being on Lester's words. For him to say that, he had to know all about the history and legends of Ouray. She hoped he would be able to fill her in on the rest of her family, too.

"You see, for centuries representatives from all the different factions of the magical realm come to Ouray to hash out their beefs and keep the peace between them and humans. I'm sure you all think I'm making this up to pull your leg, but it's all true. We wouldn't have it any other way. This year is going to be different. I can feel it in my bones. Come look me up when you get into town. I'd love to give you a tour. Don't tell the missus, but I'm really looking forward to Taboo's grand opening!"

She stopped the video and turned to the others. "There's something familiar about him but I can't quite put my finger on it."

Mark rubbed his hand over shoulder and upper arm. "Don't force it, sweetheart. It will all come to you when you need it. Click on the one labeled wildlife sanctuary."

She did as he requested and tried not to let her mind wander back to what the mayor had shared with them. Jensen's voice came through the speaker narrating a brief history of the sanctuary. She approached a group of people who she introduced as some of the volunteers. She asked them to introduce themselves and say a little bit about what it's like to live in Ouray and help care for the wildlife.

Their stories warmed her heart, especially the tale about the eagles, Elvis and Priscilla. The next participant stepped up and she clapped.

"That's Zach Nelson. He did all of Taboo's woodwork. Wait until you see the carvings he's done in the bars alone."

In the video, Zachary cleared his throat and introduced himself. "I moved to Ouray a decade ago in search of peace. My PTSD can make living in a big city paralyzing at times, but here I can breathe. Working with the residents here at the sanctuary, especially the orphan wolves, helps me pay it back, you know?"

Ian tilted his head. "Freeze the video, darlin'. We know him."

Mark's eyes narrowed a moment and then widened as he appeared to recognize an old friend. "Z-man!"

Faye crossed her arms over her chest. "Fill a broad in here. It's rude to keep all the sexy men to yourself, Boo. That goes double for the two of you furballs."

"We saw a lot of shit before we left the Corps. All of us lost friends in Kuwait, Afghanistan and Iraq. Zach lost most of his unit."

Faye put her hand over her heart. "I don't know if I could make it through that."

"He almost didn't. His PTSD can be debilitating. We lost track of him after we joined the San Fran SWAT division. Man, it's going to be good to hook up with him again."

She kissed Mark's cheek. "You'll get to say hello when we get to Ouray. He planned on meeting us to give us the grand tour himself.

He has some updates on some of the new construction on the residential part of our property."

Ian sat up. "We have a place outside of the hotel? I thought we would have digs like you have here?"

She grinned. "You can't see it from the hotel proper, but our farm house is in the northern portion of our land. It's far enough away to give us privacy, but close enough for us to be at the resort in minutes. I had this planned out well before the three of us became partners in this venture. You can still claim the penthouse suites if you want."

"No way. The house will be perfect." Ian smiled and snuggled back in with Faye.

"I hope you have my room all ready to go. First chance I get, I'm dropping in to be sure these two are taking care of you, Boo. Count on it!"

Mark laughed. "As if Tony will let you out of his sight that long."

"Who said anything about being out of his sight?" Faye fanned herself and leaned back against Ian's shoulder.

Danielle laughed outright. "We'll have room enough to spare for the three of you to plan an extended stay with us."

Ian reached across Faye's lap and tapped the remote. "Play it forward but on slow motion until you see the face of the woman standing behind Zach."

She did as he asked. Frame by frame the scene on the television moved forward. She enlarged the frame to focus on the woman. "Jesus, Mary and Joseph. That's my aunt Jessalyn. She's older of course but she really hasn't changed much at all from how she looked in my vision."

"Her smile and eyes are exactly the same. Identical to yours." Mark held her tighter against him as her body trembled.

Faye gripped her hand. "You okay, baby girl?"

She nodded. "More than okay. This confirms I have relatives in Ouray who will be able to fill in all the gaps in my memories. I'm guessing Nanny Rowan lives nearby, or at the very least Jessalyn will be able to tell me where to find her."

They spent the next hour watching Jensen's interviews and making plans to meet with her aunts and Zachary once they settled in. The guys cleared away the breakfast trays as an excuse to give her time alone with her bestie before they had to separate for the day.

"No, Ian's wolf didn't come out when we were having sex."

She opened her eyes wide. "How did you know I was going to ask that?"

"Because that's the first thing I would have asked you if our roles were reversed. I have to say, I'm glad they're not. Ian was beyond fantastic, but my heart has always belonged to Tony and Lia. I didn't realize how much until you brought us all together."

"Awww. Faye Rae. You're gonna make me cry. I didn't do anything other than help you fulfill your fantasy. You are the one who opened your heart to let them in."

Faye kissed her. "I'm going to grab my things and get out of your hair. The three of you have a lot to cover today before our girls' lunch. The men will have to fend for themselves."

She tossed back the covers and darted into her closet as soon as Faye left the room. She retrieved a gift-wrapped box she had hidden away in the back corner and shuffled in her stocking feet down the hallway. She snuck in as soon as she determined Faye was in her bathroom and placed the gift on the bed. "I have a present for you out here."

Faye gasped as she opened the garment box to reveal a purple silk floor length hooded robe. "Is this for the ceremony?"

She nodded. "I had them made for all three of us. Tony promised to have Ian and Mark in black robes to match his. At the time I had ours made, I didn't know who would be with us tonight."

"Is there anything I can do to help?"

She smiled. "You already have by being here with me. You go ahead with Ian and Mark back to your new digs. I have a couple phone calls to make to finalize the plans for tonight. Jensen and Carter will be ready to roll in an hour for our conference call."

Faye dropped the robe back into the box and embraced her. "I can't believe you'll be leaving me in three days. You've been my rock for so long. What the hell am I going to do without your face?"

She fought to keep her tears in check. This was not the time to fall apart. Both of them were headed down paths they've been praying for their entire lives. It was perfectly natural to be scared of starting out new, but now they had additional people in their lives to love and support them. "I will always be your rock, as you are mine.

Nothing will change that. No number of miles, space or time will keep us from each other. We're connected now, forever and always."

"I had this fantasy that the four of us would end up together, but now that I've seen you with Mark and Ian, I know you'll be fine. They've fallen in love with you already. Who wouldn't?"

Danielle laughed and wiped the tears from her cheeks. "I feel the same about you. Tony and Lia have loved you as much as I have all this time. We're luckier than most. We found our soul mates and have a soul family."

"Nothing better than that." Mark stood in the doorway. In his eyes, she saw the love she had for all of them.

"Ready? Tony's sent three more texts asking if I've kidnapped you and threatening to send security up to help you escape." Ian leaned against the doorframe and grinned.

Faye nodded and kissed her one more time. "We'll catch up at lunch, yes?"

"Damn straight."

The guys collected Faye's bags and promised to return as soon as they finalized their plans for the day with Tony. Both of them wrapped her in their arms and kissed her. The intimacy sent a wave of heat throughout her body, not of lust but of contentment and security.

They are your heart and soul, little one. The three of you have so much to do. Jess and I will be waiting.

*

They sat across from Tony in his office as he filled them in on the issues they had been having with a couple of the locals. Ian's jaw tightened and he gripped the armrests of his chair. Mark narrowed his eyes as he read through the private investigator's reports.

"This Don Caron is proving to be more than a nuisance. He has some sort of ax to grind with the town leaders for not recognizing his claim to our land and the estate between us and Lake Lenore. Our lawyers have cut him off at the knees and destroyed any legal claim he had by proving the documents he provided were forgeries."

Mark appeared bewildered. "He had to know those papers wouldn't pass muster. Why the hell would he take a chance like that?"

"He honestly believed what his old drunk of a grandfather had told him."

Ian snorted. "Caron is college educated. He doesn't have any legit reason to believe the claims unless he researched them himself. He had to believe someone with power would let him get away with it."

Tony dropped his pen on the desk and leaned back in his chair. "This whole thing smacks of magic. Someone, or something wants to keep us out of there, especially Dani."

He looked to Mark to gauge his reaction. "I wouldn't have come to that conclusion a week ago, but with everything that happened last night it's about the only thing that makes sense."

Mark tapped the file on Caron. "His grandfather claimed to be the bastard son of the last Jennings who owned Taboo land. He sweet-talked a lonely old man into signing everything over to him. Apparently, Old Man Jennings had been in love with one of the Brooks girls. Caron's grandfather claimed to be their love child."

"That's cold. I thought he made up the story to get out of jail for poaching?"

Tony shrugged. "That was the cover story. Caron kept up the claims. Theresa Brooks had had enough and had the courts order a DNA test. If Don had one shred of Brooks blood in him, she would have given him a share of the estate."

"Let me guess. Donnie Boy refused to be tested."

"Bingo. Instead he waited for Theresa to pass away thinking he could waltz in and have a clear shot at staking his claim on her lands."

He rolled his eyes. Caron had already rubbed him the wrong way and he had yet to meet the worm. He hadn't thought their move to Colorado would be without some hiccups, but he had hoped to have a little more time to ease into batshit crazy. "Any suggestions on how to keep tabs on him?"

"We need one of you on Ouray's town council."

He scoffed. "I'll leave Mark and Dani to fight over that. I have no interest in politics."

"Don't be so quick to count yourself out of the running for a spot. Taboo is in a unique position to be a value to Ouray. You should capitalize on it."

"I'll do it. Dani has enough to deal with. The last time Ian got political there was bail money involved."

"Not my fault. The dude was an idiot and deserved to have his nose broken."

"Dani remembered more since last night?" Tony stood to refill his coffee mug.

Ian reached for Tony's mug as he got up to pour himself another cup. "She recognized one of her aunts in a video Jensen recorded for us."

"Huh. It hadn't crossed my mind any of them would still be there, but I guess it makes sense. Someone is calling out to her to come home. Which did she recognize?"

"Jessalyn. Dani hopes to hook up with her when we get to town. The sooner she's able to piece together what happened to her as a kid, the better. You've seen the vision of the fires. Something is poised to obliterate Ouray and the surrounding towns unless the White Witch can stop it."

Mark sighed. "She shouldn't have to do this alone. We need to contact Shaman and The Crone. The two of them set us on this path. They should haul ass out here and help us sort it all out."

Tony tossed several more files on top of the desk. "These should help. My investigators have been busy collecting all you need to know on the town residents and Ouray's legends. Ask Shaman to meet you in Colorado to go through everything. I know reuniting with her aunts will be emotionally draining for her, but it is imperative The Sisters are forthcoming now. The three of you need to know what the hell you will be up against out there. Dealing with humans alone is hard enough in the business we're in."

If they hadn't already bonded with Danielle, he would have taken Mark back out on the road as far away from Ouray as possible. They had seen enough death and carnage to last several lifetimes. Leave it to them to fall in love with the savior of the magical realms. No way in hell they would allow her to face this dark power alone.

*

Instead of going their separate ways before lunch, Danielle thought it best to send Faye off for her surprise from Tony, and the rest of them meet in the main conference room for the Skype call from Colorado. Ian and Mark had summarized their meeting with Tony and their concerns over some of the unknown they had ahead of them yet. At this point, she wanted to have Tony and Lia's input to help them decide which hurdle to tackle first. Tony had smiled and kissed her when she asked him to join them.

"Where else would I be but with my favorite partner and protégé? I will be there as your advisor. The three of you have the final say in all things. You need not ask if my beautiful wife would be there for you. That goes without saying." He held out his arm for her as they walked to the elevator to the conference room floor.

Lia, Ian, and Mark had already taken their seats, and smiled as they entered the smaller of the four conference rooms on main floor. Mark got up to pull out her chair next to his. The five of them fit comfortably around the round table. "The techs left moments ago. Everything's set up as you requested."

Ian tapped the remote to tint the glass of the windows and lower the overhead lights to cut out any glare. A separate camera dropped down from the ceiling to record their faces for a videoconference.

She tapped the screen on her laptop to bring it out of sleep mode and connected to the Skype app. The red light on top of the overhead camera came on as the projection screen on the wall in front of them came to life revealing the smiling faces of Taboo II's managers. "Wow! Look at all those gorgeous people over there, Jen."

Jensen slapped the back of her hand against her husband's chest. "What have I told you about flirting during business calls, Carter?"

Lia blew both of them kisses. "We miss you sexy beasts, too!"

Ian turned toward Tony and raised one eyebrow. "Are all of our staff shifters?"

Jensen laughed outright. "You must be Ian. Tony said you would be the first to ask. I owe him a hondo. I thought it would be Mark."

"Me? Why would you think I'd be the one to ask that first?" Mark pursed his lips in a half assed attempt to hide his amusement.

"What my wife is trying to say is that she pegged you as the good cop and Ian as the one with the hard ass exterior."

Lia grinned. "She wasn't wrong about that!"

Dani held up her hands. "We'll have more time to catch up and rib each other later. Carter, why don't you fill Ian and Mark in on our staff?"

Carter's melodic Aussie accent came through the sound system loud and clear. "Our breakdown at this point in time is sixty percent shifters, twenty percent other magicals, and twenty percent humans. It wasn't planned but it does seem to work. Of course, if you feel things should change once you get the lay of the land, we'll help make it happen."

"Sounds great to me. We've been itching to be around more of our kind." Ian leaned back in his over-sized chair and crossed his ankle over his knee.

Jensen's eyes changed from green to golden amber and back again. "We're excited to have you here as well. The current guest list includes three wolf biker clubs. There have been a few minor incidents, but as soon as they heard Black and Gray Wolf were setting up residence here, they've all been on their best behavior."

Tony chimed in. "What have been their reviews of the resort so far?"

"Raves all around for the bar, club and hotel. They suggested a separate structure to house the larger motorcycles. Zach took that suggestion and ran with it. He converted two of the stables for that purpose. Let me send his pictures to you." Carter tapped on the send button on his laptop.

Dani split the screen to keep Skype active and show the photos to the rest of the room. Zachary had converted each of the buildings into parking garages for the motorcycles and their gear. Each enclosed stall had separate keycard entry, lockers and shelf space. Roof top heating and cooling systems had been installed to keep the units climate-controlled. Ian and Mark murmured their approval. She smiled and nodded. "He's outdone himself again. I found out this morning that Ian and Mark know Zach from his time in California."

"Small world, mates! We'll be sure to keep him busy on the day you arrive so you can surprise him. This has been his second home since we broke ground. He's going to be over the moon when he sees the two of you!"

Danielle glanced at her list of questions and determined most of them could wait until they were on premises. "Have there been any more issues with hunters on our land?"

Jensen sighed. "You know all about Caron's claims. He now has some twelve-year-old letter he says is signed by the oldest Jennings descendent giving him permission to hunt here."

She looked to Tony. "That one has also been proven to be a forgery."

"Exactly. The sheriff dragged him off and confiscated his guns after he *accidentally* shot at three of our guests running in the full moon last night. Thankfully, the guests chalked it up to dealing with a human off his meds."

Ian sat upright, his chair rolling backward from the table. "Accidentally my ass. You two have any idea if he has connections with a sprite or wood imp? His actions don't make sense for someone with his background."

The husband and wife team looked toward each other and back to the camera. "Something malevolent for sure. There have been whispers he has been visited by the Unseelie Queen herself as well as one of her children."

Lia rested her elbows on the table and put her head in her hands. "Queen Fitche has been itching to start a war for centuries. If she has been seen away from Court, she has stepped up her game."

"Then it's a damn good thing we came together now." Mark reached for Danielle's hand.

She agreed and wondered how long the dark fairy queen had been manipulating humans this time. Even with her limited studies with the Crone, she had learned of the utter destruction the fairy had brought down upon those who disobeyed her. No one had ever considered themselves safe around her, including her children.

"Before we let the two of you get back to our guests, is there anything else you want to discuss?"

Carter shifted closer to the camera. "There is actually. We've had an overwhelming number of requests to offer religious services, like the military has for their members."

"Multiple denominations including pagan?" Mark rested his elbows on the table and looked around the room.

"That's right. Tonight, we are lucky enough to have the head of the wolf clans preside over the Wolf Moon ceremony. All of the guests have confirmed they'll be in attendance. No one else offers this. It could help put Taboo II on everyone's radar and help us sell out years in advance."

Tony smirked but kept quiet. His eyes bore into hers, encouraging her to take the lead and make the final decision. She looked up to see Carter bouncing in his seat, practically begging her to say yes.

She laughed and glanced to Ian and Mark for their approval. Both nodded and gestured for her to give the okay. "Carter, your enthusiasm alone has our vote. You two enjoy yourselves tonight and we'll talk more about this project next week."

Carter whooped and blew her a kiss. "You've made this old dingo very happy!"

Ian stopped her from disconnecting from the session. "Hold up. How long will Hok'ee Sandoval be staying with us?"

"His stay is open ended. He said he'll be with us for as long as he's needed and that you would know what he meant by that." Jensen's eyes appeared to be troubled.

"What's wrong, Jen?" She hadn't seen that look from her before and it caused the hair on the back of her neck to stand up.

"On one hand I'm thrilled the old Shaman has honored us with a visit, but where we come from, when the Elders gather together in one place, it can only mean big trouble is headed our way."

The five of them joined hands and Jensen held Carter's. Mark spoke for them all. "We're in for the fight of our lives to protect our worlds. Together we'll face it head on. We would be honored if you joined us in battle but understand if the two of you wish to pull yourselves out of harm's way."

Both of them vehemently shook their heads. "We're not going anywhere, Black Wolf. Where the three of you are, so we will be." They raised their entwined hands above their heads and then signed off.

Ian brought the room lights back up and allowed the daylight back through the windows. His cheeks appeared flushed from the adrenaline zipping through all of them. His eyes searched her face and silently asking her if she was alright.

"Holy shit, that was powerful!" Lia rubbed her goose bump covered arms.

"Sweetheart?" Mark's eyes filled with concern.

Danielle slumped in her chair, gripping Tony and Mark's hands tight enough to turn her fingers white. The magical connection with Jensen and Carter had inadvertently left an opening in the wards she had placed around her mind. The Unseelie Queen jumped at the chance to remind her where she came from.

"They can't hide you from me forever. Whether you like it or not, my blood runs through your veins. You'll have to choose the path you'll follow, Witch."

Chapter 7

As a solitary practitioner, Danielle had never presided over a full moon ritual for anyone else. As such, she hadn't worried about what anyone else would think. She spoke from her heart to the gods and Mother Moon and had been content. Now she had the added responsibility of binding her soul to Ian and Mark. Faye had asked if she would do the same for her with Tony and Lia in the future, but after consulting with Tony, she agreed tonight would be perfect.

The staff had closed off the pool area to the guests and set up two of the large cabanas for them. The brisk night air of the desert all but ensured any curious guests wouldn't disturb them. To ensure their privacy, Tony had hired extra security to cover all access points. She didn't worry about prying eyes observing what was going on from their rooms. It wouldn't be the first time there had been naked people around the pool, nor would it be the last.

Ian joined her on their balcony overlooking the cabanas. As soon as her skin warmed from the heat of his presence, she leaned against his bare chest. His palms moved along her arms to rest over her hands. "We won't let her near you again, darlin'."

"She's right about one thing. I hate the idea that horrid creature is my grandmother." Flashes of images swirled around in her head. Nothing made sense, especially the ones with Amy and Dylan. As far as she was concerned, they were both in her past. She had meditated to clear her head to prepare her for the ceremony, and yet she still felt on edge.

"I may know of a way to relieve you of your tension." He trailed kisses along her neck.

"We have to wait…" She tilted her head back as his hands cupped her breasts.

"I'm not talking about sex, but I'd be lying if I said I wouldn't bend you over the railing and take you from behind in a heartbeat if you gave the greenlight."

She turned in his arms and placed her palm against his cheek. "After tonight, you'll never have to ask. I'll always belong to you and Mark, as you belong to me. I see an image in your mind of running."

"That's it. Connect with us while we're out. There's nothing like it. The only way you'll understand is if you experience it yourself. You can do it through our connection."

"Is that why you came out here?"

"That and I wanted a little more alone time with you to be sure this is what you want. You don't have to finish the binding. The three of us can take off and travel the world, leave all the magical realms to fight it out. You don't owe them a damn thing. We can spend the rest of our lives making each other happy."

She rose up on her tiptoes and clung to his shoulders for balance to keep her eyes level with his. "You have no idea how much it means to me that the two of you would help me escape from all of this."

"I meant every word. Mark feels the same. You know the others would agree."

"That's precisely why we can't run. We found each other because of the Prophecy. We're falling in love because of it. I won't give either of you up and if we ran, that's what would happen. Fitche won't stop until she gets what she wants. That includes wiping out all of humanity and any nonhuman who dares to challenge her. I'll be damned if I'm going to stay in hiding and in the dark any longer. If I have to go down, I'm going kicking and screaming."

He captured her bottom lip between his teeth. "There's only one acceptable reason for you to scream…"

The rush of warms between her thighs punctuated the shivers he sent through her body with his suggestion. "Oh, babe. It's going to get loud tonight!"

He groaned against her chest. "I'm grabbing Mark. If I don't leave now, I won't be able to keep my hands off you or keep Gray Wolf in check. As soon as you hear our howls, open your mind to the wolves. They'll take you for the run you'll never forget."

"Can't wait. No go. I have to finish my prep and light the candles. I expect both of you to be back at least ten minutes before the Wolf Moon's peak."

He spun her away from his body and back again. Her stomach fluttered with excitement. Dancing with him, she realized her mind had cleared out all the worry, doubts and insecurities. For the rest of the night she would devote to her soul family. "Thank you."

He kissed her with a tenderness that both surprised and thrilled her. Jensen had been right in her assessment. Ian showed the world a badass warrior, but once he dropped his armor and opened his heart, you couldn't help but fall head over heels.

She marveled at how both men appeared similar in thought and deeds but complete opposites in other ways. They were the perfect Ying and Yang. Together they completed her heart.

She finished lighting the last of the candles and purifying their space. Nothing more could be done until Ian and Mark returned. She sat on the blanket she had placed in front of her alter, closed her eyes and opened her mind.

A chorus of wolf howls reached her ears. Her concentration intensified, searching for the distinct melody of her Black and Gray.

"Join with us now, White Witch. Feel the wind swirl around you."

Black Wolf as always addressed her first. His howl resonated deep within her. Gray Wolf joined the song, teasing and caressing her spirit until the three joined as one. Her body lurched as they leapt through the air, clearing a nearby ravine with ease. The muscles in her calves and thighs flexed and extended, matching the wolves as they crossed the foothills of the mountain nearest the resort. The scent of pine filled her nostrils as her breathing quickened. The uneven path of the rocks under their feet translated back to her. Every smooth and sharp edge brought to life as if her toes encountered the surfaces. She gasped with delight, grateful for the decision to sit down before she had connected with them. She had no doubt she would have been unable to stand with the onslaught of sensations they shared with her.

"Come back to me. It's time I join with my mates, together we three."
"As you wish."

Danielle opened her eyes to find Tony, Lia and Faye had joined her on the blanket. All dressed in their ceremonial robes, their eyes glistening with anticipation. She heard them before the wolves came into view. Both bowed to her as they entered the purified area where she had draped their robes.

Faye's expression changed from happy excitement to one filled with wonder as both shifted back to their human forms. Tony stood and helped them with their robes and anointing while Danielle stood and called upon the spirits of the North, East, South and West to join them. She raised her hands, palms up and stared down at her feet and then up to the sky. "Mother Earth and Father Sky, we call on you to join us this night. The circle is cast. Blessed be."

Tony helped Faye to stand and escorted her to the center of the circle. "We call upon the Goddess to bless this woman and bring her into our family."

She held Faye's hands and began the spell to help both of them break free of their pasts and embrace their future with those who loved them unconditionally.

"Mother Moon, please grant me this wish. That the ones who hold my heart would one day yearn for me and my kiss. Sister Stars, help me plead my case. What can I do to make them see that their search can be over in my embrace? Why does my heart burn for two who cannot see? Why do they believe the love of strangers over me?"

Faye gripped her hands tighter as the words of the incantation spoke of her pain and her wish to be loved by those who had her heart. Danielle sent energy through her fingertips to boost their combined strength as the next portion of the spell would speak of their desperation to find their always and forever.

"Mother Moon and Sister Stars, guide me on my path to find a love heartfelt and true. Is that too much to ask? Please tell me what to do. I'm good enough to keep them warm on cold winter's nights, but fall short when considering a mate, a lover or a wife."

Tears fell freely down both of their faces. This had been their life up until this point. No more.

Ian and Mark joined on either side of her, and Tony and Lia did the same for Faye. While the spell would connect all of them together, it demanded they release the pain in order to embrace their future.

"Should I stay the course and hope one day their hearts will finally see that the life they've been dreaming of, searching for, is right here with me? Should I let my dream go? Let my heart try to mend? Accept the fate dealt to me and the loneliness that never ends?"

The other four moved to join hands around her and Faye, circle within a circle, to magnify the power of the spell.

"Mother Moon and Sister Stars guide me in one last Dance. I offer all I have, all that I am for one last chance. Tonight, I bare my soul for the ones whose arms I long to be in at every breaking dawn. Help me plead my case, my life, and my love. Show them that I am and forever will be, their only one."

She pulled Faye into her arms and held her close. The flames in the candles around them increased in intensity as her magic exploded out of her and into all of them. No one spoke, but she heard all of their voices at once.

"Can you hear me, my loves?"

All smiled and nodded and tried it out for themselves. Their laughter caused her heart to beat faster. This is what she wanted for them tonight, if nothing else. This was the blessing of the Goddess to begin new ventures and new lives together.

Tony reached into the pocket of his robe. "I have something for all of you."

He handed her one of the boxes and he kept the other. "I had these designed for us to symbolize our new family. Bear, Wolf, and Witch symbols combined with the heart."

She put one on each of her lover's left ring fingers. Together they placed hers. She dropped her robe to the ground to reveal her glowing tattoos; both had transitioned to their final images—her branding complete. She kissed each of them in turn. Her body hummed with the magic coursing through her, eager to join with them and begin their final transition into the White Witch and her Guardians.

Faye dropped her robe to the blanket to show her body ink. A dream catcher had been created over the middle of her upper back.

In the center of the piece they had drawn the bear claw symbol. She held out her left hand and Tony slid the ring in place. Lia presented her with a pendant with the same design.

Lia kissed Faye and took her hand. "You're the part of our hearts that had been missing. Tonight, you become our mate, lover, and wife."

Danielle faced the South and began the incantation to close their circle. She thanked the spirits and the Goddess for blessing them with each other. "By the power of the Goddess and Spirits, this Circle is undone but not broken. So mote it be."

*

Mark turned his new ring around his finger and admired the intricate design. All of their symbols appeared to glow, varying in intensity as they morphed together into one. For two years he and Ian had searched for another pack, and all along it had been here with old loves and new.

The air around them snapped and popped with the intensity of their combined magic. Danielle's moon tattoos changed to mimic the exact color of the Wolf Moon in the sky above them. Her pupils dilated leaving ink black pools, pulling him into their depths. Black Wolf panted and paced.

Ian tugged at the sash around Mark's waist, freeing his robe from his body. His hands moved up his chest to his face. He and Ian had been lovers since their teens, but never had he felt this close to him, the intimacy caused his body to tremble and ache with need. His cock swelled and his lips parted as Ian's lips met his.

Danielle moved to stand behind him. Her hands moved over his hips and around to wrap around his body. The cool skin of her breasts crushed against his back did nothing to soothe heat zipping through his body. Instead, the contact stoked the fire between them. His desire for both bordered on obsession. She kissed and licked his shoulders and his neck as Ian's tongue danced and swirled around his. He moaned and surrendered to their embrace.

The rest of the world fell away as they moved to the cabana. His eyes adjusted to the candlelight as he drank in their surroundings. The king-sized bed in front of him had been covered with pillows and sheepskin blankets. In a corner near the head of the bed he noted platters of food and drinks. She had thought of everything to make their celebration complete.

She smiled and knelt up on the bed. She reached for both of them. "Tonight, I give everything I am and will be to you. Our lives will forever be entwined. Nothing will keep us apart ever again."

He kissed her as Ian moved to the bed behind her and positioned the pillows in the center. She clung to him as he eased her back against the down filled cushions. She sucked on his tongue as Ian latched onto her left nipple, circling the nub with the tip of his tongue.

Mark snaked his way down her body, kissing, licking and tasting every inch of her along the way. Ian knelt at her head as she wrapped her fingers around the shaft of his cock and swirled her tongue around the tip. The sight alone sent a jolt of electricity through to his core. He parted her thighs further and dipped his tongue between her folds. She raised her hips up to his mouth, offering her pussy to him. His lips sealed over her clit as he stretched her with two and three fingers.

Ian groaned and thrust his cock into her mouth as she stroked his shaft and massaged his balls. "Fuck me...don't...stop."

Her back arched as her body convulsed. Cum shot out of her and coated his fingers. She tasted sweet and salty, of wine and strawberries and he wanted every drop. His fingertip rimmed her anus, coating it with her cum. He inserted one knuckle at a time, waiting for the ring of muscles to relax with each advance.

"Mark..."

He glanced up her quivering body. His eyes locked with hers. Her chest rising and falling rapidly. Black Wolf howled.

He slid back up her body and pinned her arms up over her head. His eyes never left hers as he plunged his cock into her. He ground his pelvis against hers, rubbing her swollen clit. Her cunt spasmed around his dick, bringing him in deeper and deeper with each thrust. Her tits bounced wildly as another orgasm tore through her. A rosy blush moved from her breasts, up her neck and her cheeks.

Ian tore open one of the condoms and covered his cock. He moved behind Mark and stretched his ass with lube-covered fingers. The bed dipped as Ian slid into position. Mark let go of her hands and braced his arms on either side of her. She moved her hands up over his arms and eased his body down over hers as Ian inched his cock into his ass.

Gray Wolf joined with Black Wolf. Their combined song signaled the end of their lonely quest. White Witch was theirs at last.

He relaxed his body and yielded control to Ian. With each thrust into him, he moved inside of Danielle. She lifted her legs higher around him to rest her heels against the side of Ian's lower back. The three of them moved together, higher and higher until they broke free of the last of their inhibitions. They cried out for each other as their shared climax shot through them.

The interior of the cabana exploded with light. At the center of it, stood a woman in flowing royal blue robes and long wavy auburn hair streaked with white. She spoke to them through their minds.

"At last, our White Witch is one with her Guardians. Wolf, Witch, and Fae together again. The Elders are gathering, awaiting your arrival."

*

Ian and Mark dropped to the bed on either side of her, both panting. Even though mere inches separated her body from theirs, an overwhelming sense of loss washed over her. She wondered if this was what it was like for an addict jonesing for their next fix.

Ian turned toward her and propped his head up on his hand. "You've never had that with anyone else? Ever?

She turned her body toward him. Mark spooned against her back. "You heard that?"

"No. Not the words but your emotions. Before we could sense them, now we share them."

Mark nodded and rested his cheek against hers. "Everything is magnified threefold."

"I've never shared anything remotely close to what we have now." She entwined her fingers with theirs over her hip.

"Was that the Crone who projected herself here?" Ian slipped his arm under her head and inched closer to her and Mark.

"Yes. It's unnerving how my aunts show up in my head like that."

"We had this discussion last night in the club. Sex is powerful magic in of itself. Your binding kept your family from finding you until now. I'm guessing when you surrender control during an orgasm, your mind lets them come through." Mark rubbed his stubbly chin along her bare shoulder and neck.

Her mouth watered and her nipples hardened to the point they ached. This was their night. Everyone and everything else could wait. She lifted her right leg over Ian's hip and rolled them over to bring him under her.

Mark chuckled. "Our girl knows what she wants."

"Both of you, always."

Ian sat up and crushed her breasts against his chest. "As you wish."

Mark steadied her hips as she lifted up from Ian's lap. He reached between then and guided the head of his cock into her opening. She sighed as she lowered herself to encase all of him. Mark kissed her neck and shoulders as his hands roamed from her hips to cup each of her tits. He squeezed them together to match the rhythm she started. She raised herself up, nearly lifting off Ian's dick completely then back down again.

Ian closed his eyes and tilted his head back. Her lips moved from his mouth, over his chin, and down to the sweet spot behind his ear. He moaned as her tongue trailed down his neck. No longer able to continue the slow pace she started, she pushed him back against the pillows. She braced her hands against his chest to give her extra purchase as she moved her hips forward and back, forward and back. His cock caressed every sensitive spot in her pussy sending ripples of ecstasy through the three of them.

Mark's cock appeared to pulse with need for her and Ian. He guided her forward until her nipples brushed against Ian's chest. He coated his fingers with the lube and resumed stretching her tight anus. "Relax, sweetheart."

She moved off Ian's cock enough to reposition and give Mark access. His fingers teased and feathered her until satisfied she was ready. He grabbed one of the anal toys from the box next to the bed and covered it with the lube. He replaced his fingers with the toy.

"Ohhh…" The sensation of having both her cunt and ass filled sent her body quaking. Ian hugged her close as Mark worked the toy in and out of her. Her pulse quickened in anticipation of having both of her men inside her at once.

Mark sheathed his cock with a condom and lifted her hips up. The head of his cock slid between her ass cheeks. Her thigh muscles trembled against Ian's legs.

He kissed her forehead and both cheeks. "Hold on to me, darlin'. Don't move until he's all the way in."

She stared into his eyes and bit her lower lip as her ass muscles stretched to fit around her lover. Mark's upper body lowered until his chest touched her back, his lips brushed the back of her neck. He slid his cock out an inch at a time and back in over and over. Her cunt spasmed wildly around Ian's dick. He pulled her mouth to his as her passion reached the peak once again. Mark's body stiffened as Ian thrust up into her and filled her with his seed.

She buried her face against Ian's neck and slid her hands over Mark's braced on the bed. "Don't move, yet."

"Honey, we're going to crush you."

Ian moved his arms around her to hold Mark still. "A moment longer, please."

Mark's cheek rested against the middle of her back. In this position, the three of them were perfectly entwined. Skin on skin on skin. Their hearts synced with each other until they beat in unison. The last of her memories broke free from the place where they had been locked away. Her voice projected throughout the magical realms.

"I am the one foretold, born of Seelie and Unseelie blood. I wield the magic of my ancestors and tame the wild beasts. We were kept apart for centuries, but are now one mind, one heart, one soul. I am the White Witch and these are my Guardians."

Chapter 8

Their last days in Nevada had flown by, but somehow, they had managed to pack and arrange for most of her things to be shipped to their farmhouse. The few pieces of luggage on the bellhop cart had been all she determined to be her necessities. Nothing else mattered as long as she had Ian and Mark by her side.

Faye had refused to drive with them to the airport. "I don't like ugly crying and if I have to watch that plane take off with you in it, I will fall apart."

"I love you, Faye Rae. Take care of Tony and Lia for me."

"I love you too. Before you know it, we'll be all be together bringing the kink to Colorado."

The limousine pulled around to the entrance of the hotel. Tony and Lia caught her up into a double bear hug. "You sure you don't want us to go with you?"

She shook her head. "Faye needs you both. She has the right idea about ugly crying. It's hard enough leaving the three of you now."

Lia hugged her again. "You need anything, magical or otherwise, we'll be there."

"That goes for me, too."

She spun around to find Cameron in his Sunday best. "You didn't think I'd let my best customer leave without saying good-bye, did you?"

She threw her arms around his neck as he lifted her off the ground. "I think I'll miss you the most, Scarecrow."

He laughed. "Now you've gone and quoted my favorite movie. What the hell am I gonna do without you to run interference with the other bitches?"

She kissed both of his cheeks. "Don't ever change, Cam."

He turned to look both Ian and Mark up and down. "I won't as long as you tell me where to get me one of those."

Ian winked. "That can be arranged."

Cameron's laughter rang out with that of the others and it warmed her heart. Now, she could leave knowing they would take care of each other. The driver opened the door as she approached. She lowered her head to take her place and froze. There seated in the center of the limo sat Jessalyn and Rowan. Their nearly identical smiles broke out as soon as their eyes met hers.

Rowan's eyes sparkled with mischief. "Little birdy told us you might be needing a lift to the airport and Jess was tired of waiting for you to make it to Ouray."

"What are ya waiting for, an engraved invitation?" Jess patted the seat next to her.

She turned back to gauge Ian and Mark's reaction to the additional riders. Both appeared to be as surprised as she was. She shrugged. She guessed she should have expected as much after she sent out their introduction to the Universe.

Ian and Mark slid in behind her. Jess appeared to be fascinated by their tattoos. "Ohhh! They shift. I didn't know humans could do magic like that. Do you have any that do that, Dani?"

She knew what her aunt was trying to do there with the question. "I covered my scars years ago. None of our tats were done by humans."

Rowan nodded. "Told you so."

Jess rolled her eyes. "Don't be a smartass, Ro. We don't know what Eileen did to hide her from us. You can't blame me for asking." Her Iris brogue triggered additional memories of all four of the sisters ribbing each other. She giggled before she could stop herself.

Rowan clutched Danielle's hand. "I've waited so long to hear your laugh again. I can't believe Fiona talked me into sending my granddaughter away."

She patted Rowans hand and shook her head. "That's in the past. We're together now."

Jess put her hand over theirs. "Aye, that we are. We have so much to talk about and so little time. I hope you don't mind we hijacked your travel plans. The Elders thought it best to hit the ground running. We can get started as soon as we're settled on the plane."

"I'll take a guess and say you've cancelled our original flight plans?" Ian chuckled. He appeared to be enjoying himself.

Jess's mischievous grin caused him to bust out with laughter. "I have a few connections in that department. One of my charges has graciously put his Cessna and its crew at our disposal. We can trust all of them. The Elders made sure of that."

Normally the ride to the airport from Elko took less than ten minutes, but it seemed to stretch out as her anticipation grew. They were finally going to get some answers about her past and what was expected of her as the White Witch. She knew the Prophesy and the riddles associated with it, but at last she would be able to understand how it all applied to her, Ian and Mark. As promised, their plane had been fueled and cleared for take-off as soon as they arrived. Danielle had worked with Taboo clients to secure charters so she knew all the paperwork involved. Tony had planned on one day securing a plan for the resorts. After checking out this one, she made a note to ask him about securing more than one. Mark agreed with her.

"Plenty of leg room in this model." He tested out the reclining feature with his seat and scoped out the couch seating the sisters settled into.

Rowan's eyes locked with Mark's. "I know you like your naps when you travel, but for this we're gonna need your full attention. Do I make myself clear, handsome?"

He smiled, took her hand in his and kissed it. "I'm all yours."

"What about me?" Ian didn't bother to keep a straight face. He appeared to be enjoying their company.

Jess elbowed Rowan. "Move over, Ro. I want that stud muffin to sit next to me."

Danielle grinned enough to cause her cheeks to ache. She enjoyed watching her lovers flirt and sweet talk her aunts. While she had been taken aback to find them in the limo, now it seemed perfectly natural they would be there ready to prep them for what they were about to face in the months ahead.

"Hand me that bag, would you Ian?" Jess pointed to an oversized tote in the storage area for the mini-bar.

He retrieved the tote as she asked and whistled. "What the hell do you have in there?"

Jess laughed. "Stop teasing. It's not that heavy. It's Dani's grimoire. We've been keeping it safe for her and filling it with all the spells and invocations she's going to need to ascend to her position as Judge of the Realms."

"I have my grimoire in the trunk. It's the one Fiona had me start when I trained with her." She peered into the tote and the book's magic called to her.

"This one is extra special. The Elders of the Realms contributed to this so that you have all the knowledge you need to be a fair and impartial Judge."

"Who has served in that role until now?" Mark's moved to sit on the other side of Danielle to get a better view of the book.

Rowan sighed. "Up until Dani was born, it had been a group of six Elders: two from the Fairy Courts, Witch, Human, Angel, and Wolf. All had agreed at that last gathering their representative would continue to rule in your steed until you came of age."

"Everyone except the Unseelie Queen. She demanded you be brought before her and tested to determine your true lineage. She refused to believe her eldest son and run off with a Seely princess." Rowan's eyes darkened and her face turned red with anger.

Ian placed his hand over hers. Danielle sent her love through him to her. "What happened to my parents, Nanny Rowan? Why did their union create so much strife between the Fae?"

Rowan pointed to the grimoire. "All the answers are in there but I'll tell you this. Fitche has always been unhinged. From her first days on the Court to the day she tricked the Unseelie King into declaring her his queen, she's been plotting to take over everything."

Jess opened the book to the first pages. "Whatever you seek, speak it out and the book will tell you where to find it within its pages. You can study Fitche when you're safely back in the protective boundaries of Ouray."

"It's okay, Jess. I can speak of Aithne and Phalen now. It's time she knew how much they sacrificed for her to be born."

Danielle leaned against Mark for support. She had known both had died, but not that she had been the cause of their deaths. Mark turned to give her more contract with his body. She noticed Rowan had turned her hand to grip Ian's for strength to continue. He nodded to her.

"I have her, darlin'. Her whole body is quaking. This is something she's not shared with anyone besides her sisters."

"There isn't a law against Fae from fraternizing between the two Courts. Generally, we stick to our own so to speak, but sometimes the planets are aligned and a love of the ages is born. That's what it was like when my Aithne met Phalen the Red Phoenix."

"Like Romeo and Juliet." Ian encouraged her to continue.

"Exactly. Some on both sides vehemently opposed their union. Fitche forbid Phalen to claim Aithne as his wife. The most vocal one who stood against them on the Seelie Court had been Eileen."

"I'm not surprised. She's been a bitter person as far back as I can remember. The fact she refused to tell me about my mother clinched it for me years ago."

"Don't be so hard on her, dear heart. She wanted to protect her niece from the same humiliation and broken heart she had suffered at the hand of the Unseelie King."

In her mind that didn't excuse the actions of the woman who she had thought of as her only living relative. Being told day after day you were worthless and an albatross around your grandmother's neck would tear anyone down. Danielle had refused to take it any longer and had jumped at the chance to spend her summers and then all of her free time with the Crone. Finding out she was her Aunt Fiona had put everything in perspective.

In their own way, each of the Four Sisters had given her the building blocks and tools to grow into the woman she was today. "So Aithne and Phalen ran off together. I assume that didn't go over well with Fitche."

Jess shook her head. "No, it didn't. She had her minions capture and torture him. Still he refused to tell her where Aithne hid. At that point, she had already given birth to you. He gave his life to protect both of you."

Danielle shook her head in disbelief. "Fitche killed her own son? What kind of monster is this creature?"

"The worst kind. She has always been willing to sacrifice anyone and anything that stood in her way to rule all of Mother Earth, not only the Fae. The Unseelie King couldn't care less what she does as long as he is left alone to do as he pleases."

"Phalen wasn't his son?" She would never treat a child of hers or any in her care the way these beings have done.

"No. All four of the phoenixes were sired by another prince of the Court. Phalen the Red had been the oldest and the favorite of them all. His brutal death rocked all of the Realms but no one stood up to Fitche. She placed a bounty on Aithne's head and that's when the Witches of the Seelie Court took action."

She listened to Rowan detail what had happened to her as an outsider, completely detached from it all. It turned out to be the best way for her to absorb the information, without crumbling in a heap on the floor of the limo. Her mother had dropped her off with Rowan in the hours before dawn.

"I had begged her not to go. We would be able to protect her from anything Fitche sent our way, but she had refused. Her heart and soul had shattered the moment Phalen perished. She had nothing left to give let alone raise you with the love you deserved."

Mark's arms encircled her body as she turned to hide her face against his shoulder. Ian got up to kneel beside them. He hugged both of them close. Jess slid over to give them room and hold Rowan's hand.

"Danielle, that was the last time any of us ever saw Aithne. I know in my heart, she is alive. Fitche's bounty has never been claimed."

"How could she stay hidden all this time when Phalen couldn't?"

Jess answered for her sister who appeared overcome with emotion. "He allowed them to find him in order to give your mother the chance escape. Her power had been the ability to shift into any animal, bird, or reptile. We believe she may still be in animal form and living in the mountains surrounding Ouray. Now you're on your way home, she may find it safe to show herself again."

The thought her mother may still be alive filled her with determination to find her and bring Fitche to justice. If the Unseelie Queen could destroy members of her own family, then no one is safe as long as she is in power. She hoped the Elder Grimoire would give her the ammunition she needed to end the strife within the Magical Realms and wipe Fitche off the face of the earth.

Ian helped set up the tables so they could spread out. Jess provided them all with yellow notepads and pens from another of her large tote bags. Danielle smiled to herself. She inherited Jess's organizational skills. Her own office had stacks of notepads she used along with her tablets and smart phones. No doubt she and Jess were going to work well together in Ouray.

Rowan reached into her own bag and produced a moon amulet. "I gave this to your mother when she came of age. She placed it in your bassinette to protect you. Fiona and Hok'ee added additional charms to symbolize what you have now become."

Danielle covered her mouth with one hand and held the amulet in the other. The charms were separate representations of the tattoos on her hips. Full moon, Black Wolf, Gray Wolf, Celtic Knot, and Pentagram all present and accounted for on the chain. In the center of them all, a charm of three hearts, entwined to form an infinity symbol. "How?"

"We've been waiting so long for the three of you to come together. Each of the charms had been forged centuries ago and held by the Elders of the Wolves, Witches, and humans until now. So, if either one of you have any doubts that you are the answer to the Prophecy, I hope this puts those to rest."

Mark helped her secure the clasp of the chain around her neck. As the charms settled against her chest, they emitted a soft pink light and a faint tinkling sound of chimes floated around them.

"I guess that's settled. What's next on your agenda, Jess?" Ian clicked his pen but kept his eyes locked with Danielle's.

"Don't ya love a man with a purpose?" Jess winked and handed him a list.

Ian grinned as he scanned to items. "Shaman will have us busy as soon as we check in. Jensen was right. Multiple Wolf Clans are heading to Ouray. The leaders of the Realms are gathering as we speak."

Jess turned to Danielle. "There are few who know you are my niece, but most will not. For your protection, it's best we don't advertise it. We'll be seeing each other all the time with Ouray business so it won't seem odd that we're fraternizing. My duty has been to watch over the Hawkins and Brooks families. From their families we have the human guardians. We lost the last of the Brooks descendants last month. We're waiting for the Guardian Healer of the Arrow to find their way back home. More of that history is in your Grimoire. Just know, I will be there for you always, in person this time."

Jess handed Mark another list. "Tony happened to speak to Mayor Ross on your behalf concerning a spot on the town council. Consider it yours. There will be a few who will protest for all of fifteen seconds, but since I adore you already it's a done deal. Lester will do anything to shake up the council for the better. We need to keep the diversity we've always had in Ouray. If that balance is removed, it will open the door for Fitche and her ilk to destroy it once and for all."

Mark scanned his list and placed it on the table in front of him. "It's true that Ouray has always been the gathering point? It seems odd that there has been no other spot on the planet where magic can reside in peace with humans.

"Everywhere there are wildfires, magical worlds collide. Emotions run high with our kind and as such things tend to get heated. Sometimes that heat will smolder or rage out of control. The same goes for how we show love for each other."

Danielle's cheeks warmed. She had experienced that kind of passion with Ian and Mark. It made sense to her that others would experience the same kind of fire with their soul mates. The thought that the same emotional inferno could be used against others of their kind scared her. Anger was one thing, but what they faced now could end up in death and destruction of entire races.

Rowan passed her a bottle of water. "What the three of you share is a blessing in and of itself. It's part of what will save us all. There are dark times ahead in the coming months. Taboo will be at the epicenter simply because all Realms know they are welcome there."

Danielle added a few more notes to her pad and glanced around the table. "We started House of Taboo with that in mind. It was only natural we continue that policy with this one in Ouray. I hadn't realized until the last couple days how important it was to continue with that mission."

"It's what convinced Mark and me to accept Tony's offer. Looks like our compulsion to search the world for our kind wasn't wanderlust. I thought Jensen's comment that we were famous was simply friendly ribbing, but the wolves are gathering because of us."

"Aye. Those you've encountered in your past, are traveling to Ouray to witness your ascension. You started that with the Wolf Moon ceremony. Fiona and Shaman will complete it on the next full moon. The Snow Moon. This year it falls on the last day of January and into February." Jess took her water from Rowan and gulped down half of it.

Rowan stood and moved to sit next to Danielle. She handed her an engraved invitation announcing to the Realms the ceremony would take place on the Brooks estate near Lake Lenore. "It's also the Blue Moon when the Crone moves on and she passes all she's learned on to the White Witch. You will be able to tap into all the magic of the universe. You see, this is your time. All you've been through up to the moment the three of you came together has prepared you for this."

She moved her fingers over the raised lettering over the thick vellum. "If all of this would have started a month ago, hell even a week ago I would have run for the hills. No way would I have ever felt I could handle all of this. I'm ready to tackle all of it head on. How can I lose? I have all of you and so many more in my corner I've yet to meet."

Ian raised his beer and the others followed with their drinks. "Where you go, we go. Fitche has no idea what she's unleashed."

Jensen and Carter brought the new Taboo stretch Hummer limo. With the new snowfall, it was the best choice for the forty-minute ride south from Montrose Airport to the resort. Plus the expanse of windows afforded her the chance to take in the winter wonderland. She'd been surprised to learn the snow they were seeing now had been the most they've seen since Thanksgiving.

"They're saying it's the lowest snowpack level in at least three decades. They're worried it's going to bleed into spring leaving our area in tinderbox conditions." Carter pointed out how the top of the nearby mountain appeared more brown and green than white."

Mark sighed. "We say this happen in Cali too. Mount Shasta looked barren for at least four years. It affected more than the immediate surrounding areas. The entire state declared drought conditions. Mother Nature handed Fitche the perfect backdrop for her attack. If she uses her dragons and the remaining phoenix loyal to her, she could devastate everything within six states of Colorado in less than a week."

"I've already started to gather provisions for fire season out at Hawkins Ranch. What would you say if you offer Taboo's storage area to house evac supplies?"

Danielle didn't need to be asked twice. The idea appealed to her on multiple levels. Not only would it give them an in with the town residents, it would give her an excuse to spend more time with her aunts. "We have plenty of room in the storage barns near our house at the back of the property. We can start organizing the space any time."

Jess scribbled away on her notepad while Jensen tapped away on her smartphone. Carter laughed and called them twinsies. Jess rolled her eyes and peered at him over her readers. "You should be so lucky to have the two of us on your arm, Carter. Don't you forget it."

"I would be honored to escort both of you to the ascension ceremony."

Danielle snickered. "I don't think Ian is going to let you horn in on his date."

"You got that right." Ian draped his arm around Jess's shoulders. She giggled and pretended to work on her list while a nice shade of pink spread over her cheeks.

With each mile they traveled, her soul lightened and a sense of welcome washed over her. Her mind opened to the voices calling out to her, happy to have her back home.

"Welcome home, White Witch. The Angels are honored to be by your side."

"The Wolf Clans add their voices to welcome you back home, Witch and Wolves."

"The Creatures of the Mountain and Forest welcome their Queen home. We are at your service as always."

"The Witches of the Seely Court welcome their long-lost daughter back into the Coven. You're as radiant as ever, little one. We cannot wait for your ascension."

She opened her eyes to find everyone watching her. Jensen and Carter's faces filled with wonder, while Ian and Mark smiled. Rowan and Jess wiped happy tears from their cheeks. All had heard the messages sent out to her. They looked to her for guidance when it was she who needed them to show her the way. A surge of energy coursed through her body and lifted her confidence to take the reins of the role she had been born to take.

Her first decision would be an easy one. She wanted to roll up her sleeves and dive right in. As the rustic mountain resort came into view, her pulse quickened and the magic sparked between her fingertips.

"Let's get this party started."

Chapter 9

Mark leaned against the bar and watched the band they had hired for their grand opening rehearse. The lead singer, Derek Quartermarsh had impressed him from the moment he and Ian caught one of his shows in Vegas. The dude easy on the eyes and had the talent to back it up. With his band, Quarter to Three, he had scored a major recording deal after their virgin tour. When not touring, he spent his time designing tattoos and creating masterpieces for all of the Saints and Sinners nightclubs. Mark hoped to commission pieces for Taboo.

Aidan Phoenix dropped down on the stool next to him. He had arrived in the wee hours of the morning and apparently hadn't been to bed yet. "You were right. This band is kickass."

He smiled. "Don't worry. Your job is secure. Quarter to Three is here for the grand opening weekend. You're to be our regular entertainment. That is if you keep your dick in your pants."

Aidan grinned. "Not my fault the chicks toss their panties and their room keys at me. What am I supposed to do when it's offered up to me like that?"

"All I'm saying is watch yourself. Our clientele is a mix of human and non-human. We don't need Dani to have to intervene when you fuck an Elf pledged to marry another."

Aidan's right hand turned to purple flame. "I can handle myself with the non-humans. I'm here to protect Dani from my mother. No amount of pussy will change that."

Mark placed his hand on Aidan's shoulder and the flame died away. "I didn't mean to suggest otherwise. Ian and I are grateful you're here now. After the opening, we have to prepare for her ascension. She doesn't know you're here yet. We wanted to surprise her, but maybe you should see her face to face now?"

He hung his head. "I've done a lot of things I'm not proud of since she was born. Not standing up to my mother from the beginning is the tip of the iceberg. Dani isn't the only one I have to make amends to while I'm here."

"Seems to me you were royally screwed over. Your brother is butchered in front of your eyes and you're forced to give up the love of your life. I think you deserve a bit of forgiveness from whomever you feel you wronged. I can say with all certainty, Dani will feel the same. She wants to connect with all of her family if possible."

"How about we meet up for lunch? I need a shower and a little shuteye before I see her. Last time was when she was a wee thing that fit in the palm of my hand. Phalen told me I'd fall in love with her and he was right. Soon as that tiny hand latched onto my thumb I was a goner. The photo of her up front in the lobby damn near knocked me off my feet. She is the perfect mix of Aithne and Phalen. Those eyes of hers? All Phalen."

"Sounds good. Come up to the suite at one."

Aidan shuffled off toward the elevators as the band ended rehearsal. Derek joined him at the bar and shook his hand. "This place is out of this world. I'm going to have to bring my fiancé out here. That is if I can tear her away from work long enough."

"I hear that! You let me know when you plan to be here and we'll give both of you the VIP treatment."

"We've stayed at House of Taboo a few times and loved it. It's good to be able to stay somewhere we can be ourselves."

"Speaking of that, my partners and I would like to commission some of your art for this place when you have the time."

Derek tilted his head to the side and smiled. "I get to incorporate the magic here too? Like how your tat shifts?"

Mark almost spit his coffee out over the bar. He hadn't expected Derek to be one of them. "You can make ink come alive, too?"

Derek nodded. "I get a little help from my Guardian Angel. Say the word and I'll do some mock-ups for you. That's something I can do on the road."

"It doesn't bother you to be around so many non-humans?"

"Are you kidding me? I live in Vegas, brotha. They're all non-humans in that city!"

"You got me there. Good to know we have another ally."

Derek excused himself to get some down time in before his performance, leaving Mark alone to run through the lineup for the party one more time. Without the music playing in the background, his mind wandered to all that they've accomplished in the three days since they arrived in Ouray. Jess and Rowan had dropped them off at Taboo to get settled in. It had taken most of the afternoon and into the evening to meet with the staff and run through the plans for the grand opening kick off party. Dignitaries from all over the world had clamored to be on the guest list. The rooms had booked up within minutes of them coming available. He had never been a part of anything like this. He had felt like a fish out of water when they first started their meetings, but Jensen and Carter made him feel like an old pro within the first hour. With the team they had assembled, he was confident the opening would be a success.

This stuff he could control, or at least bluff his way around enough so others thought he knew what he was doing. His connection with Dani helped in that regard. All of her knowledge was available to him at any time. All he had to do was tap into it. He preferred the old-fashioned way for business and their mind-speak during their private time.

"Hey, babe. We missed you at breakfast." She folded him in her arms and kissed him.

"I woke up before sunrise and couldn't fall back to sleep. I caught Derek's rehearsal. The band has really gelled since Ian and I saw them last."

"He tell you about his Guardian Angel?"

"How the hell did you know about that?"

She flashed a sheepish grin. "We might have had a few conversations over margaritas when he and Sarah stayed at the House of Taboo. I had actually forgotten all about it until he checked in last night."

"He happen to tell you he's game to do the artwork for us?"

She clapped her hands. "Yay! I was hoping he would say yes. With his talent to bring his models to life in his murals, we'll be able to incorporate protection spells all throughout the resort."

"The thought had crossed my mind the minute he said he could see my tattoo shift."

"We need all the allies we can get from the human world to make our plan work. The Elders are set to arrive next week. They want to meet and go over the ceremony. Queen Fitche has refused to participate but her husband has already agreed to send his representatives in their place."

The hair on his arms stood on end as his flesh covered in goosebumps. "Any idea who they will be?"

"Only their names—Seamus and Cael. They're princes of his court and two of his most trusted advisors." The look in her eyes set off warning bells in his head. He tried to read her thoughts, but all he could see were swirls of color.

His stomach clenched. They very well may be his advisors but no way in hell he trusted them. This was his way of disrupting the proceedings and rip out Aidan's heart even further. "Sweetheart, I don't know what the hell is going on, or what sort of cruel joke the Unseelie King and Queen are playing. Seamus and Cael aren't ordinary advisors. They are two of the last phoenix brothers and your uncles."

She closed her eyes and filled her lungs. As she slowly let out the air she opened her eyes. Her pupils had dilated and her skin turned ice cold. "If they think for one minute I'm going to fall apart at the sight of my father's brothers, they've made a grave mistake. I know all about them thanks to my Elder Grimoire. Let them come. I'll hear what they have to say and then send them packing."

"Damn, woman. You know what it does to me when you get like this."

She took his hand and led him away from the bar. "Yes, I do. There happens to be this elevator fantasy of mine I'd like to relive if you can pencil me into that busy schedule of yours."

He lifted her up in his arms and walked toward the private elevator up to their suite. This time he meant to ride up and down that thing until she begged him for mercy.

"You read my mind." She bit his lower lip and set his wolf free.

*

Every muscles and bone in her body had turned to jelly as Mark made good on his promise. She had begged him, not for mercy, but to never stop loving her. Until that point, they hadn't come out and said they loved each other. Maybe they had thought it too soon to declare those exact words, but how else could she explain what she felt with both of them. Her declaration of love for him had stoked the fire between them to another level. As her body surrendered to him, her mind opened and transported them to another realm.

Mark kissed her eyelids. "Where did you bring us?"

She opened her eyes and smiled. He held her with her arms and legs wrapped around his body as they floated in the warm salt water. "The mermaid caverns. Jensen said they'd completed the enchantments yesterday."

"Danielle?"

She turned her focus back to her lover. His eyes bore into hers. His expression turned from surprise to one she had thought she'd never see again. He had fallen in love with her as fast and furious as she had with him and Ian. Her heart beat faster wanting to hear him say the words but afraid she was reading too much into it.

His lips sealed over hers and she melted again.

"You don't have to say—"

He kissed her again to silence her protests. His hands moved up and down her back. Her skin tingled and heated at his touch, in spite of the cool water swirling around them.

"I love you. First Ian saved me, and now you. I barely existed in this world until we found each other."

"You are the one who holds all of us together. If you and Ian hadn't let me into your pack, I would have stayed lost. Your dreams led both of you to me. You may be my Guardian, but you are Alpha for our family."

"I love both of you too, but you really have to give a guy a little warning before you take him along on your wild ride."

She grinned. *"I didn't hear you protests during our breakfast in bed."*

"I'm not complaining at all. A heads up would be nice especially when I'm in the middle of a meeting with Carter. Shaman will be here shortly and I don't want to have to explain my monster hard on to him. You know how he is."

Mark laughed. "Take us back, sweetheart. Ian's right. Hok'ee Sandoval is all business with no time for the pleasures of the flesh. He sees it as a weakness."

She snorted. "Sex is and has always been the most powerful magic for all of our kind. But I can see his point. Sex can also be used as a weapon and distraction to keep us from our paths."

She closed her eyes and concentrated on transporting them back to the elevator. Mark's tongue snaked along her neck as she returned to her body. No longer pinned in the corner, she stood in his arms in the center of the lift. Her head buzzed with the residual vertigo sensation. She reached around him and pressed the button to release the elevator. The doors opened into their suite. Thankfully, Ian and Carter weren't there to greet them.

He shook his head and smiled. "You'll have no problem winning him over."

She narrowed her eyes. "Maybe he's the one who has to win *me* over. I mean, between him and Fiona, we've been kept in the dark about what we're supposed to do here."

"True. He's the Elder of the Wolf Clans. As such, Ian and I must defer to him. You, however do not. You do you. Rumor has it he and Fiona go way back." He winked.

They walked through the living room, down the hallway and into their spacious master bedroom. She had designed it to match her suite back in Nevada including the walk-in closet. She stripped out of her clothes and chose another outfit more appropriate for the meetings they had planned for the day. Mark did the same. She smoothed her hands over the body hugging V-neck sweater as he slipped is down over his chest. The deep shade of purple had always been one of her favorite colors. Without even trying, the two of them had chosen coordinating pieces of clothing.

He zipped up her sweater dress and kissed her bare shoulders. "I love when you wear halter type dresses."

"Is that so?"

"Bare arms and shoulders are a major turn on."

"For me too." Ian smiled from the doorway.

She sat down and laced up her knee-high patent leather boots. She would save the thigh high versions for the party tonight. Her eyes took in Ian from head to toe. He chose dark smoky gray dress pants and a wine-colored button-down dress shirt. "How the hell and I supposed to concentrate on anything today with the two of you looking so hot?"

Ian kissed her as she stood from the bench. "We'll have plenty of time to feast on each other again later. We have a lot of ground to cover today before the celebration kicks off tonight at nine. Thanks to the influx of celebrities, the press has been swarming all over town. There isn't a vacancy anywhere from here to Silverton."

She smiled. "I would expect nothing less. Taboo II has the benefit of feeding off an existing reputation. It's up to us to make sure we live up to the hype."

"I'd say a three-day party should do the trick. I guess I would have preferred not to have so many people around so close to your ascension." Mark picked up his laptop and followed them out of the bedroom.

Ian's phone buzzed on his hip. "That would be Carter. Shaman has asked to meet with the wolf clans in the main ballroom."

She raised an eyebrow as they entered the elevator. "When did that meeting change to wolves only?"

He put his hands up. "Don't shoot the messenger, darlin'. I found out less than an hour ago myself. The Clans have always been in charge of security when the Elders gather. My guess is Shaman wants to touch base and confirm all will be on point."

"Shouldn't I be involved in any discussion concerning the ascension?" She swallowed to remove the lump in her throat. She had had enough of being kept in the dark and wasn't about to allow her Guardians to do it to her, too. If they wanted to keep secrets from her now, they had better not bitch when she did the same.

She crossed her arms over her chest and took a step away from both of them. She faced the doors and tapped her boot, willing the doors to open. Ian folded his arms around her and pulled her back against his chest. He lowered his head to rest his cheek against hers. Guilt flooded through her. She hated it when others turned into divas and here she was escalating to launch into Super Bitch on steroids. She turned in his arms. The steady rhythm of his heart beating soothed her frayed nerves and the tension left her body.

"I'm sorry. I shouldn't have snapped at you."

"It's understandable. We have a shit ton of things to get through with Taboo alone. I promise you Shaman is in no way trying to keep secrets from you, and neither are we. There are just so many things one person can juggle at a time. You have to let your teams do the jobs you hired them to do. As for everything else, Mark and I are as much in the dark with the rest of the realms as you are with the Wolf Clans. It has been a very steep learning curve for the three of us but together we can figure it all out."

She tilted her head up to look into his face and reached for Mark to join their circle. "I need to know that no matter what happens, we won't keep anything from each other for very long. I can't ask you to promise to never keep a secret from me, but please don't keep me in the dark indefinitely. I'm much stronger than I look, you know."

She moved out of Ian's arms and held up both of her hands, pinkies out.

Both men laughed and hooked their fingers with hers.

She rose up on tiptoe and kissed both of them. "Pinky swear oaths can never be broken. They can bend, but never break. That's how I feel when I'm with you." The door opened to the lobby streaming with people. She watched her men weave around the guests and workers toward the hallway leading to the grand ballrooms. She sighed and turned her attention to the front desk. Every customer service representative appeared to be busy with check-ins. No one manned the checkout line.

She smiled as that sunk in. No one manned that designated section of the front desk because no one wanted to leave. She walked through those waiting to be helped introducing herself and answering any questions about the resort.

"I heard that you all specialize in orgies." The middle-aged woman's eyes widened as her voice dropped into a whisper.

Danielle smiled. "Is that one of your fantasies?"

The woman's face turned fire engine red and she nodded.

Danielle took the seat next to her and held the woman's hand. "Think of this place as Fantasy Island. If your idea of a hot night is sitting in bed eating chicken wings and watching the Super Bowl, then we can help make that happen. If you wish to explore your most secret desires, you've come to the right place."

The woman leaned forward. "Is that what the contract is for? Secrecy?"

She nodded. "It's to protect you and the other guests. The most important rule here is there must be consent from all parties. Everything is discussed ahead of time to be sure that if you or any other participant feels uncomfortable in any way, the fantasy scene is ended. No harm. No foul."

The woman's companion pulled his chair closer. "What if we do have an orgy fantasy, hypothetically speaking?"

She smiled. "If that is your true desire, we can help you explore that but there are some taboos we consider forbidden and will not happen anywhere here at this resort."

Two other couples joined their circle of overstuffed chairs. Danielle signaled for additional chairs to be moved closer to them. "Here at Taboo and our sister resort in Nevada, we do not allow fantasies involving bestiality, the exchange of money to engage in your fantasy with you, the use of illegal substances, or the use of anything that is against the law in any state of this country. There will never be anyone under the age of twenty-one here at any time. No exceptions. What we offer here is for consenting adults."

She looked around the small group. All eyes filled with wonder and excitement of choosing the first of what she hoped would be many fantasy fulfillment requests Taboo would bring to life for them. She stood and signaled to two of the representatives to come over and help their guests with check in. "I hope to see all of you tonight for our party. I hear we're in for one hell of a magical event. You might catch a celebrity or two on the dance floor."

She excused herself and headed toward a group of guests seated on the benches around the marble fire pit in the center of the entryway. The wooden benches had been hand-carved with Native American symbols of fertility, love, and life. She traced her fingertips along the carvings and smiled at the memory of Zachary Nelson showing her his illustrations of the carvings. His enthusiasm for the entire project had been what clinched the job for him six years ago. He had been there with her every step of the way and brought every vision, no matter how small, to life.

"I didn't think I'd be able to see you here this morning."

She turned to see the very man she had been thinking of. She hugged him and kissed both of his cheeks. "Jensen said you wanted to stop by this morning. How could I turn down a chance to catch up with you?" She looped her arm through his and led him back to her offices down the hallway to the right of the front desks.

"I wasn't sure when the three of you would get settled into the house, but I assumed you would be here this weekend to be close to the action."

She laughed. "That would be an understatement. Ian and Mark have hit the ground running. You would think they've been managing resorts for decades. I for one can't wait to sleep in that beautiful cherry wood bed you built. You've outdone yourself, my friend."

He smiled. "It was my pleasure to surprise you with that. If it weren't for you, I wouldn't have the business I have today. The bed is a small gift. Whatever you need, all you have to do is ask and I'll do my best to make it happen."

She turned her head to the side. "What about you? When are you going to fill me in on your greatest wish?"

Sadness crept into his eyes. "I'm afraid I may have lost my chance at a happy ever after."

"Never say that. Love is never lost, but sometimes it's put away for safekeeping until all parties are ready to receive it."

"Do you really believe that? Even if years go by before they see each other again?"

"Who is she?"

He stammered. "How...how can you tell?"

"Call it women's intuition. Spill it. You know I'll get it out of you eventually. If you don't, I'll have to bring in my secret weapon."

His eyes widened. "You wouldn't."

"Damn straight I'll go to Jess. You know she'll spill your secret in a heartbeat."

He slouched in his chair, crossed his ankles and gripped the armrests. He told her everything—from their first contact after her grandfather's funeral to their whirlwind weekend together. They had promised nothing more to each other, and yet his heart longed to be with Callista Hawkins again. His biggest regret had been leaving her bed for his flight back to Colorado. "I've been trying to get up my nerve to travel back to Seattle."

"Have you tried to contact Callie again?" She reached out to his mind, not to read his thoughts but feel his emotions. He loved her; that much she caught from his body language and the fact he had gushed about her nonstop. In his heart, she picked up his fear Callista would reject him if she ever saw him at his worst. Every other person he had ever cared about before he had moved to Ouray had bailed on him the first time his PTSD incapacitated him.

"I've started at least a dozen letters and emails but ended up deleting them. She has stayed away from Ouray because of her grandfather. I'm a constant reminder of him. He was my best friend and I still grieve for him. I understand her pain. How can I ask her to push that aside?"

Images flashed through her mind on fast forward. She saw everything he spoke of as if she had been present during all of it. She sensed Callista's fear of giving herself to the one man who ever understood her heart and soul. Danielle heard the veterinarian's voice as she cried herself to sleep asking that Zach not give up on her. Callista loves him and yet she's battling a darkness that keeps her from giving her heart to him again. She silently promised to do everything in her power to get the two of them back together.

"As soon as you are able, get your ass to Seattle. At the very least, send her another letter. Reach out and ask for another chance to show her how much you love her."

He smiled. "You saw a bit of our future when you touched me, didn't you?"

She grinned. "Let's say both of you are due for your happy ever after together. Stop waiting and grab it."

He stood and kissed her cheek. "I'll keep that in mind. You've given me hope. Once we get through the winter, I'll clear my schedule and take a chance."

"Callie is like you. She has buried herself in her work. That can't go on indefinitely. Something has to give."

He bit his lower lip. "Sometimes losing yourself in work is the best way to cope with the darkness."

She held both of his hands. "Ian and Mark told me a bit of what you go through every single day. I want you to know, I'm happy you're in my life. When those voices and nightmares attack you, tell them you're under the protection of the White Witch and her Guardians."

"You're serious, aren't you?"

She nodded. "You've witnessed the magic here with your own eyes. The old myths and legends are true. Every single one of them. Listen to your heart and let the magic flow through you."

His eyes glistened. "I wish it were that simple, but I promise you I will try to do as you ask."

She closed her eyes after Zachary left her alone and reached out to his ladylove. She had only been able to connect long distances with magical beings, but Callista was a Hawkins. Her place was in Ouray representing the Human Realm.

"It's time you return home, Guardian Healer of the Arrow. Ouray and Zach need you."

Chapter 10

Shaman Hok'ee Sandoval strolled into the packed ballroom as impressive as ever. Besides the streaks of white running through his long black hair and the beginning of crow's feet near his eyes, the man appeared the same as the day Ian first met him as a kid. Without speaking, the Navajo medicine man managed to bring all eyes in the room to him. All eagerly awaited his direction. As the Elder of the Wolf Clans, it's his word alone that determined how they would interact with the other magical realms. Some of the younger shifters had caused a commotion when they checked into the resort, demanding to be taken directly to Shaman. Thankfully, the person at the desk had set them straight before the Elder had arrived. If the pups had continued, Ian would have been forced to ban them from the resort. He couldn't risk anything interfering with Danielle's ascension.

While Mark had his hands full with the entertainment for the evening, he had taken on the task of rounding up the clans for individual debriefings prior to the arrival of their leader. In his experience, Shaman's patience wore thin rather quickly, and he would prefer not to have anyone get on the old man's shit list early on. Seeing the satisfied expression on Shaman's face was enough to tell him the debriefings had served their purpose.

"Thank you all for journeying far and wide to be with us for this historic occasion, Next week the White Witch will ascend and take her rightful place as the Judge of the Realms. By her side, as always will be two of our clans as her Guardians. Black Wolf and Gray Wolf will at last return to their rightful positions and receive the Gift from the Elders."

Ian's eyes locked with Mark's. *"Gift from the Elders? Did you know about this?"*

"No. This is a new development. The Prophesy never mentioned this."

The entire ballroom erupted in loud murmurs and some shouted questions. It appeared he and Mark weren't the only pack members left in the dark on this. He focused his attention back to Shaman Hok'ee at the center of the podium. He held up one hand and all silenced again.

"We are on the brink of war with the Unseelie Queen and her supporters throughout the Realms. Some of them are in this very room. If that's your path, you would do wise to leave this place and never return. If we find you stayed and you continued your betrayal, there will be no trial. Your life will be forfeit."

He had never heard Shaman speak this way and he sure as hell didn't expect to see three dozen wolf shifters stand from their seats and calmly leave the room. Carter nodded and followed them out to be sure all were escorted safely from the property. If word got out they had traitors within their ranks, a full-on blood bath would erupt. Admitting they had chosen Fitche ensured their honor would remain intact. If they had kept up their deception, there would have been no safe place in Heaven, on Earth or in the worlds in between for them. They would become the hunted.

He didn't recognize any of those who left but he would be damn sure to have their names from Carter before lunch. Danielle would want to know she wouldn't be able to rely on all wolves to have her back. He hoped The Sisters might be able to help create a detection charm to help them recognize the wolves that had turned.

"Now for the rest of you. This is to be more than an ascension ceremony. It's also the transference of power from the current Judge and her Guardian to their successors. To ensure a smooth transition, all of you will need to be present and form the Circle of Power around Lake Lenore. There are six of you here today who were present for the last ascension and I am grateful you have kept the secret. Today, you are released from your oath of secrecy in order to prepare the others for what is about to take place."

Movement at the side of the stage drew Shaman's attention. He smiled and held out his hand. The woman on the receiving end of his smile reached for his hand as she joined him. Her face radiated pure joy and happiness at the sight of him.

If Ian were a betting man, he would have laid odds this gorgeous creature was Shaman's soulmate. By the looks of her red hair and familiar smile, she would have to be the mysterious Fiona. She was nothing like what he had pictured in his mind for how The Crone would look like if he met her in person. Even her projection hadn't done her justice. His heart hammered in his chest for she bore a remarkable resemblance to Danielle.

"No wonder we feel so close to the Sisters."

"I agree, but there's something else. Look at the way he protects her. I can't believe we hadn't figured it out before now. Shaman is the current Guardian, White Wolf."

"We will continue that discussion later, boys. My niece will want to hear all of it and I'd rather not have to repeat everything twice. No, Hok'ee cannot hear us at the moment. I'll tell him about this later before we see Danielle."

"I am Fiona Brautigan, the Eldest of the Four Sisters, The Crone, the Purple Witch and the Judge of the Realms. The time has come for my reign to end and that of a new era of peace and rebirth to begin. In order for that to happen, we must eliminate the scourge from our midst. Everything Fitche has touched, she has corrupted, mutilated and destroyed. She has brought nothing but pain and misery to all of our worlds. I've asked my Guardian to help me in this last task and bring the White Witch into her full power. I give all of you the same choice. Will you stand with me one last time?"

"Aye!" All stood and voiced their vote. Not one of them refused her. Ian turned to face Mark to see him grinning from ear to ear. He shook his head and rolled his eyes. He wished he had his partner's innate ability to read a situation and figure out every possible outcome. He had to admit it did make for some interesting investigations while they were on the police force together. That's what made them a great team. They balanced out their weaknesses and strengths.

One thing bothered him with the entire exchange they had witnessed. Why did Fiona only have one Guardian? The legends all speak of the Judge having at least two. Did they lose one or more of their family? His stomach rolled at the thought of losing Mark or Danielle. How could Fiona and Hok'ee go on without them?

Shaman slipped his arm around Fiona's waist and kissed her cheek. "The Wolf Clans have agreed. We will protect you now, forever and always." The couple walked out together into the shifters and greeted many by name. Ian had never seen his mentor this way. Fiona appeared to bring out the best in him. If this is what Danielle did for him and Mark, then he looked forward to every single moment.

*

Danielle looked up from her desk as Darby Shaw tapped on her door. The owner of the local brewery had promised she would stop in after delivering their order of her pale ale. "How's the last-minute prep going?"

She got up from her seat and hugged the sassy brunette. "I've decided to stop fretting and let it play out. I can't be everywhere at every moment, so fuck it."

Darby laughed. "That's the spirit! I can't wait to see what you have planned tonight. I see you snagged Quarter to Three. Their fans have taken over my bar. Not that I'm complaining!"

She laughed. "Win-win for all of Ouray. You don't know how happy I am to see you now. What would you say to joining a few others and me for a girls only spa session to get ready for tonight? I figured all of us work hard during the week to keep our businesses running smoothly and we could use a little pampering."

"Are you serious? That would be a big yes for me."

"I was hoping you would agree." She handed her a small gift bag.

"What's this?" Darby peered inside.

"Part of your VIP experience. You'll find all you need to access your room here at Taboo. I can't have you all worn out running back and forth. You'll want to stay the all three nights."

"This is too generous."

She held up her hand. "Sister, please. You've gone above and beyond to welcome us, not to mention supply Taboo with the pale ale. It's our bestseller. Besides, I miss having friends around to do the girly things with. Ian and Mark are sexy as hell, but they're not exactly the spa day types."

Darby grinned. "I don't imagine they are. The two of them must keep you rather…uh…busy. I've always wondered what it would be like to be the center of a man-sandwich."

"Are you asking for yourself or for a friend?" She winked and smiled.

"I've read some of those ménage romances but not sure how it all works out, you know."

"Between the three of us, there wasn't any awkwardness. We were already part of the lifestyle. When it's a new exploration, communication is the key. It starts with the attraction, then the connection, communication and then finally the manifestation of all your wildest dreams and fantasies."

Darby's cheeks turned bright pink. The blush enhanced her beauty. Danielle sensed the other woman never thought of herself as stunningly beautiful. Tonight, she would be damn sure to help her see it. "If you aren't comfortable talking to our fantasy coordinators, I can help make it all happen. If your fantasy for the next three days is to be pampered twenty-four-seven, with or without the sex, we have you covered."

"In that case, I better get rolling and finish the rest of my deliveries. I have to pack my bag and officially check in for my Taboo experience."

She hugged Darby again and told her she expected to see her in the suite at four sharp. That would give at least two solid hours of pampering before she had to get ready for the kick off dinner with the other VIPs. Her stomach growled as she glanced at her watch. "Noon? Where did the morning go?"

She gathered her notes and shoved them into one of the totes she picked up from the gift shop. She had forgotten to grab her brief case when she left the suite and didn't feel like running back up for it. Instead, she spent the morning chatting up the new guests, checking on the menus and going over some of the new fantasy requests. Carter had stopped in to drop off a thumb drive for Ian. He had been rather tight-lipped about the contents saying only that it pertained to the Wolf Clans and he was sure Ian would fill her in. She dropped the thumb drive into the tote's zipper pocket for safekeeping and headed toward the private elevator to the suite.

Jensen joined her on the way. "Darby left all smiles. I take it she'll be joining us this afternoon?"

"That would be a big yes. You should have seen the way her face lit up. I wish I had extended the invitation sooner. No matter. She'll be checking in within the next couple hours. Could you have flowers and champagne sent to her room as a welcome and send a car to pick up Jess and Rowan at the Hawkins Ranch?"

The other woman nodded and scribbled away on her tablet. Somehow, she kept pace with her on the marble floor without tearing her eyes away from the screen. The rhythmic tap-tap-tap of their heels on the shiny surface brought her one more bit of comfort. Taboo II had already become her home. She looked forward to the down times in their farmhouse, but it was in the thick of the action where she was in her element.

"Oh, one more thing. The kick off dinner is to be a private affair with the Mayor and his wife, Darby, and the other business owners of Ouray. The rest of the restaurant is open for our guests. No paparazzi. I don't care if they have a letter from the President of the United States, they aren't getting into the building."

"We've already had to have the sheriff escort a bunch of them off the property. Should we add in additional security on top of the extended group we have now?"

"You tell me. You and Carter were at the meeting of the Wolf Clans."

"I...I don't want to speak out of turn."

Danielle sighed. She had no intention of going through the secrets bullshit again. Once all the craziness of the coming week was over, she planned to have a serious sit down with everyone. "We hired you and Carter because you are highly qualified and trustworthy. Just because we're on site now, doesn't mean you have to run every single thing by us. I'm not asking you to divulge any secrets handed down to you from your Elder but if he feels we need extra security, then I trust his judgment. If *you* have a gut feeling we need additional manpower to keep uninvited nuisances out of our hair, then by all means, girl, jump on it."

Jensen smiled and visibly relaxed. "Consider it done."

The elevator doors opened and she stepped inside. "Good. Now do what you have to do and get your ass to the spa at four." Jensen saluted and turned her attention toward a commotion at the front entrance. A new wave of guests had arrived in need of her expertise. Danielle leaned against the back of the elevator as she observed her manager step up and take charge of the entire check in process for the new arrivals.

Her stomach rumbled its protest that lunch wouldn't be served until one. If she timed it right, she'd be able to raid the fridge for a quick snack to hold her over. She stepped out of the car into their entry way and nearly collided with Mark holding a parfait glass filled with yogurt and berries.

"I heard your stomach rumbling."

"Seriously?" She narrowed her eyes and reached for the dairy treat.

He moved the glass out of her reach and captured her lower lip between his teeth. "Ian said you only had toast and tea this morning. Lia told me you have a nasty habit of immersing yourself in work and forget to eat."

"Have I told you how much a love you, yet today?" She widened her eyes and batted her lashes.

He laughed and handed over the yogurt. "I love you too, babe. There is another reason I'm bribing you with food."

"Ha! I knew it. What are you trying to butter me up for now? Has Shaman decided to add another Guardian to our family?"

He visibly paled. "No. Why would you think that?"

She placed the glass on the table along with her tote. She slid her arms around his neck and kissed him. "Honey. I wasn't thinking it at all. It was a piss poor joke. With everything that has been tossed at us lately, that seemed like the most absurd thing I could think of to say. That's all."

"There are more shocks in store for us today. The next one will be arriving at one. It's one of your father's brothers."

"I thought you they weren't due to arrive yet." She picked up the yogurt and headed toward the couch. She scoped up several berries with the yogurt and spooned the mixture into her mouth. She closed her eyes and sighed.

"Not Seamus or Cael. It's Aidan."

She sputtered and nearly inhaled a blueberry down her windpipe. "Where did you find him?"

Mark combed his fingers through his hair; a gesture she had come to learn meant he was about to admit he's been keeping secrets.

By the way he shifted from foot to foot, it must be a more than a little white lie. She patted the cushion next to her and waited for him to spill it.

"Remember the entertainer Jensen said she found in New York, the one who can mimic any voice, male or female?"

"Yes. She said he reminded her of one of my favorite acts in Vegas. Danny Gans. He was da bomb! Broke my heart when he died. Never thought there would be anyone else like him."

"Aidan Phoenix is our opening act tonight and will be one of Taboo's featured performers. Jensen had no idea who he was when he signed the contract. He's here to protect you from his mother."

"You've talked to him already?"

He nodded. "This morning while the band practiced. Aidan arrived while you were asleep. I asked him to meet you then and there, but he wanted to get some sleep himself and build up the courage to see you in person."

She slid into his arms and pulled her legs under her. "What makes me so scary that people need to steel themselves to meet me face to face?" She wasn't joking around this time. One of her uncles had traveled to see her and yet had to collect himself in order to look her in the eye. What did he have to hide from her that she didn't already know or couldn't find out all on her own with the Elders Grimoire?

"I think they're anxious you'll be able to read what's in their hearts. Some have secrets locked away that are too painful for them to relive again."

"Are you speaking from experience?"

"The pain of losing our pack leader two years ago sent me reeling. I almost lost Ian then too. I don't ever want to go through that again. You made that pain bearable for me. Now I can talk about it and not be afraid of losing myself to the grief."

Love surged through her. "You do the same for me. I don't think I'd be able to handle the rush of memories and magic returning to me. The two of you help me more than I will ever be able to express in words."

He leaned back so they could stretch out. The top of her head settled beneath his chin. She loved it when he held her this way. With his arms around her, she let herself relax and mold her body to his. The soft material of his sweater brushed against her skin and allowed his body heat to warm her. The sound of his heart beating soothed her frayed nerves and lulled her into the quiet place in her mind.

His hands moved up and down her back rubbing and massaging every knot from her muscles. If she could stay there with him the rest of the day, she knew without a doubt he would make it happen. Ian would do the same.

"You'll both be here when Aidan comes up, right? I mean—"

"We'll be in the kitchen, waiting for your signal. Unless you want us to be in the room right from the start."

She lifted her head and he turned to look her in the eyes. His appeared full of the same swirling emotions in her heart. His eyes reflected everything she felt inside and so much more. "Let's play it by ear. I'm still sorting out the memories from my childhood that came flooding back the night we met. Maybe he holds the key to unlocking more."

His palm caressed her cheek. "I wish I could be of more help in that department. I can feel your frustration."

"You are what I need to get through it. Having you and Ian with me is enough."

"Speaking of our lover. He wanted me to wake him when lunch arrived. Seems a certain someone wore him out this morning. He said he needed a nap to be able to bring his A-game for his date with Jess tonight."

She laughed and sat up. "You know he made her year asking to be her escort. Jensen and I have reserved the private room at our spa to pamper the hell out of her and Rowan."

"Ian and I have a surprise planned for you ladies while you're there, and no we won't show up and ruin your girls only party. We wanted to add to the pampering. This is a big night for everyone and we want to it to be one you'll never forget."

She crawled back on top of his body; dropping kisses over his neck and chin. Her lips sealed over his. "I can't wait."

"You make it damn hard to think of anything else but making love to you all day."

"Are you complaining?" She nibbled his ear lobe.

"Hell no, but if we don't stop now, Aidan is going to have a front row seat while I enjoy my dessert."

"You make a good point. Go before I change my mind." She kissed him one more time and let him slide out from under her. She closed her eyes and curled up with one of the couch pillows. Ian wasn't the only one in need of sleep. A good twenty-minute power nap had been her go-to midday pick me up in Elko. She thought it would be a good idea to put it into her daily planner and make it one thing she would do for herself without fail. She snorted at the thought. She would be lucky to be able to pull it off two days in a row. She fluffed the pillow and closed her eyes to enjoy the moment and let tomorrow take care of itself.

*

Aidan paced outside the suite, working up the courage to knock. Nothing scared him more than the thought Danielle would send him away and blame him for the loss of her parents. He had been sworn to protect all three of them, but Phalen had sent him away with Aithne and their child. Aidan had been the only one his brother had trusted to protect his family.

He relived those moments in his nightmares. The frequency of those horrible visions increased on the anniversary of his brother's death, the night of the Wolf Moon. His mother had always taken pleasure in perverting the sacred rituals of the Fae and the Witches. He shouldn't have been surprised she would choose that night to destroy the one son who had loved her unconditionally.

After he had settled Aithne in her hiding place, he returned to his brother's side to find he had been too late. His brothers, Seamus the Blue and Cael the Green had Phalen bound between two Weeping Willows. Fitche wielded a cat o' nine tails with barbs dipped in poison. With each strike, she tore away her son's flesh. The poison seared the wounds enough to slow the bleeding but not the pain. Slash after slash she mutilated his back, turning his skin and muscle to purple jelly.

Phalen never screamed, never begged for mercy. His silence infuriated Fitche.

She held out her hand. The Captain of the Queen's Guard placed the Fire Machete in her palm.

The weapon created to destroy a phoenix.

"No! I beg of you. Don't do this!" His plea had echoed throughout all of the Fae Realms and yet no one came to their aide.

111

She had turned to him, eyes black as night and cold as ice. "Save your breath or suffer the same fate. He is dead to me and now he will be dead to us all."

She slashed through his body with long, vicious strokes. As Phalen's body fell apart, it burst into red flame one last time, fully combusting.

No ashes remained for the Red Phoenix to rise again.

The door in front of him snapped open and pulled him out of his horrific memories. Danielle stood in front of him, her face a mask of grief. She launched into his arms and held on to him. Her body trembled as she cried with him.

He wrapped his arms around her waist and returned her embrace. "I didn't mean for you to see that. I forgot how powerful you have become."

He placed her back on her feet but held on, afraid to let her go. Afraid she would disappear like she had done in his nightmares so many times before.

She slid her hands up to the sides of his face. "I remember you, Aidan. I remember your smile and your laughter. I thought for years you were my father. You look exactly how I remember him."

"You were barely six months old. How do you remember?"

She wrapped her fingers around his thumb and he melted on the spot. He guessed some bonds are never broken no matter how much time had passed. "My Little Lynx has grown into a beautiful woman. So much like your mother, but your eyes are like your fathers and mine. As I told Mark this morning, I would know your eyes anywhere."

"Nothing in the Elder Grimoire prepared me for seeing you here in the flesh. They said you were lost. No one has seen or heard from the Purple Phoenix for decades."

Sadness washed over him. "That's a story for another time. First we have to get you through your ascension."

Her face paled. "Seamus and Cael are due to arrive next week. The book goes into great detail about those two, but no mention they had a hand in murdering my father."

"I should have guessed they would try to show up here now that you are out in the open. They are not to be trusted, you hear? It was their treachery that lulled Phalen into thinking they would protect him from Fitche.

Ian and Mark had slipped into the room and waited for them near the seating area. Ian's fists clenched. "No way in hell those two are coming anywhere near, Dani."

She led him toward the sofas and urged him to sit next to her while Ian and Mark took the seats opposite. "They are representing the Unseelie King, not Fitche. Protocol dictates they are allowed to speak. We don't want to risk alienating all of the Unseelie because of their chosen representatives."

"Don't feel sorry for the lot. They have a choice, like the rest of us. Seelie or Unseelie doesn't matter. It's the Dark and the Light they chose. Both Courts are made up of dark, light and a bit of the gray. Humans tend to see it as Good and Evil, but you and I know it's much more than that. Fitche and those who follow her are the blackest hearts around. She has followers within the Seelie as well."

"And with some of the Wolf Clans. That's what the meeting was about earlier. Those who chose Fitche, were asked to leave now." Ian's angry posture told him he wanted to hand out his own brand of justice to those who would do her any harm.

"Leave now and keep their honor as warriors. That is the Wolf way is it not?" Aidan's eyes focused on Ian's face.

"It is, but it doesn't mean I have to like it." Mark placed his hand on Ian's shoulder. Their contact eased his tension, but not his determination to keep close tabs on those who left.

She focused her attention on her uncle. "It seems we have even more to discuss before my ascension. I'll trust your judgement with your brothers. I'll not call them uncles. I refuse to acknowledge them as family. You on the other hand have given me back a piece of my heart I thought was gone forever."

"I've never stopped searching for you even when Fitche held me captive. I had hoped you had come into your phoenix power along with that of your mother's powers. Now I know why. As White Witch your flame will burn brighter than all."

*

She placed her hand over his. "What are you saying?"

His eyes widened in surprise. "I thought Fiona would have taught you how to harness the flame by now. Maybe that's why I'm supposed to be here. I can be your tutor. Never thought I would teach my Little Lynx how to flame out."

Mark leaned back in the cushions. "Was that her nickname as a baby?"

Aidan nodded. "Aithne had the ability to shift into the most beautiful lynx in all the Realms. She had been looked upon as the successor to the Queen of the Forest Creatures. That's how we hid the two of you, as Momma Lynx and her kitten. The creatures hid you as one of their own until your mother brought you to Rowan."

"All of this happened here, in Ouray?" Ian leaned forward, his interest piqued and his anger over the wolf betrayal placed to the back of his thoughts.

"Aye. Where else? This is our home and has been since the dawn of time. We may travel this world and those in between, but we always come back to Ouray and the mountains that protect it."

She hadn't read any of that in the grimoire at this point but would dive into the volume the first free moment she had. The shock of having such a vivid vision take over her mind had literally brought her to her knees. The moment she was able to stand she had opened the door. She had no way of knowing if the vision had been real or a ruse to get her outside of her suite, but she took the chance anyway. Moments before, Mark had told her that her uncle would be joining them for lunch. He held a key to unlocking more of her memories and she had been anxious to see him. Aidan had stood there in the flesh, a piece of her past and now her future.

"It's not only your magic from your witch ancestry that gives you the spark in your fingers when you cast a spell, love. That's the phoenix fire. It's part of why you're so powerful. You are a mixture of all parts of the Realms. Witch, Fae, Human and Shifter with a touch of Angel. That's what a phoenix is you know. Fallen Angel and Fae."

Her cheeks burned. She had a few sexual encounters with the Fallen, both male and female, and had enjoyed every moment. Maybe the attraction she had had for them had been due to her own bloodlines and not fantasy fulfillment.

A knock at the door signaled their lunch had arrived. Ian excused himself to take care of the set up. Mark waited until he was out of the room to speak. "Both of us were shocked when the wolves stood to leave. Carter confirmed all of them were from the same pack. Their leader is one that has started to build a reputation as a troublemaker. We didn't recognize any of them because all were recently turned. None developed their shifter ability as kids."

Bile rose to the back of her throat. "These shifters aren't natural born?"

Aidan sat back against the cushions and closed his eyes. "Fitche has been experimenting for centuries to create an army of non-humans. If what you say is true, she's reached the point we've all feared. Her minions could infiltrate every realm and destroy it from within."

Mark nodded. "That's why Shaman Hok'ee called them out this morning. It culled the Clans and sent out a warning to any others who wish to follow in their footsteps."

At the mention of the medicine man's name, Aidan's body stiffened. His eyes changed to a deep violet. His hands shook in his lap. "He's here? Hok'ee Sandoval is alive and well?"

Danielle placed both of her hands over Aidan's and gasped. He opened his mind to her the instant their skin connected. She saw an entire village engulfed in flames. Aidan's screams echoed throughout the canyon. She could see everything through his eyes; feel everything he touched and how it burned his flesh. Her body lurched with his as he fell to his knees and allowed the purple fire to consume him.

She returned to her body, kneeling with Aidan on the floor. He placed his hands on either side of her face. His thumbs brushed the tears from her cheeks. Mark and Ian stood at the ready to jump in if needed. "What happened to those people, Aidan? Who burned their village?"

"They said there was one who survived that holocaust. One woman who was able to describe the murderer of her family and tribe to the authorities. All this time I thought Hok'ee was lost in that fire. It was his family who were killed so I assumed—"

"The one you loved was taken as well?"

Aidan inhaled sharply and appeared to be taken aback by her question. "His...His granddaughter and I...she was my life. I can't talk about her now. Please. It hurts too much." He covered his face with his hands and sobbed.

Her heart shattered. He had witnessed the destruction and deaths of all he had loved at the hands of his mother. How he had held himself together at all amazed her. "You don't have to talk about any of it now. I don't know about you but I could use a bite to eat to help clear my head. What do you say?"

He smiled through his tears. "You are most definitely your father's daughter. He would always use food to cheer me up. I'm sorry to come here and take you to such a dark place. That wasn't my intention."

She hugged him. "I know. Promise me that when you're ready you'll share all of your story with us. We're family. We stick together through good times and bad. Now that you're back in my life, I have no intention of letting you disappear again."

He stood up and helped her to her feet. "You get that bossiness from your mother's side."

Mark snorted. "I have to agree. Jess and Rowan are a handful all right."

"They've got nothing on Fiona. I had thought she would be here with you. She is the one who found me and said you had come out of hiding."

Ian cleared his throat. "She is here but wanted you to have time alone with Dani first. After what you've shared with us so far, I would say she had the right idea."

Danielle nodded. She had so much she wanted to discuss with Fiona, but Aidan took center stage now. Through him she learned more of what her parents sacrificed in order to bring her to this point. The thoughts of running away from her destiny turned to determination to fight.

Chapter 11

Ian and Mark had followed through on their promise to make the day memorable. While the women sipped champagne, the seamstress from Taboo's boutique brought in three racks of gowns and all the accessories to match. Rowan and Jess helped each other pick out their gowns, while Jensen assisted Darby in narrowing down to one from the three that had caught her eye. Danielle wasn't given any other options. Her men had taken the liberty of deciding for her. Everything from the lingerie to the shoes fit her perfectly. She gasped as the assistant unzipped the dress bag to show her the gown.

The deep plum velvet material hugged her in all the right places and the split bateau neckline bared her shoulders. The delicate lace overlay shimmered with tiny crystals that enhanced the form-fitting bodice. The long sleeves ended with a point of lace at the back of her hand. She stepped into the four-inch plum pumps and moved in front of the triple mirror. The high-low hemline gave her the elegant evening dress she wanted plus sassy enough for dancing all night long.

Rowan joined her in the mirror. "You take my breath away. The boys know you well."

She smiled. "That they do. Seems to me they were spot on with the rest of you too."

Jess twirled around in her emerald green satin. "I feel like the bell of the ball. If he wasn't already taken, I would snatch Ian up for myself."

Rowan laughed. "Good thing our girl has his heart. You would wear the boy out!"

The room filled with laughter as they finished dressing. They had managed to spend a full two hours with massages, body waxes, nails and hair. At the point the dresses arrived, all of them appeared content to stay in their fluffy robes and slippers until they had to go up to their rooms. Ian and Mark's surprise had enabled them to stay together another hour. Darby excused herself to meet with the mayor and his wife for drinks before dinner and Jensen followed in order to help Carter get into his tux.

"It's time we show our dates how lucky they are to have us on their arms tonight. They're waiting for us up in the suite."

"Guess again." Rowan smiled and pointed to the door behind her. There stood Aidan, Ian and Mark dressed to the nines in black tuxedos with pocket squares that matched their dresses.

Jess giggled as she slipped her arm through Ian's. "Eat your heart out ladies. Me and Stud Muffin will try our best not to steal the show."

"Oh, you hush yourself! My date is performing tonight so we'll see who will be stealing the spotlight."

Aidan grinned from ear to ear and kissed Rowan's cheek. "I've missed you, lass."

"I've missed your smile. Makes my heart sing to see it again."

Mark placed his hand over his heart and gazed into her eyes. "I've seen you like this in my dreams, but nothing could have prepared me for this moment. Ian, you were right. The purple did me in."

Ian winked. "I knew it would. Come on. Our dinner guests are waiting and the night is only beginning." He kissed Jess on her neck and set her off into another fit of laughter.

Danielle took Mark's arm as the six of them left the spa and out to the main floor of the resort. Deep mauve carpet had been rolled out over the marble floor from the entrance to the restaurant and the nightclub. Ushers dressed in purple and hot pink leather stood along the route, eager to assist with final check in preparations. As promised, Jensen had secured the additional manpower to protect the property and check that all who arrived at the front doors had their invitations in hand. Even the guests currently staying at the resort, had to produce their invitation or be escorted back to the elevators to their room. Not one of the guests had complained about the extra security and seemed to welcome it.

The paparazzi and the hundreds of Quarter to Three fans, as well as Aidan's female admirers were not as understanding. The sheriff had to place checkpoints on the highway at the entrance to

Taboo's property to keep the traffic moving along out of town. That hadn't stopped some of the more resourceful party crashers. A group of college aged locals tried to use the Brooks' estate to sneak in the back way. They didn't expect the ring of wolves blocking their path.

None of that mattered now as they entered the private dining room in the restaurant. Besides Mayor Ross and his wife, the owners of all Ouray businesses had accepted their invitation. Darby stood from the table and pulled her aside.

"I don't know how you did it, but all of the town council is here too. I've never known them to agree on anything but all of them have raved about Taboo so far." She peered around her and her eyes widened. "Is that, Aidan Phoenix with Rowan? How did you manage to keep him under wraps all this time?"

Danielle smiled. "Family connections. He's performing tonight and most nights for the foreseeable future."

Darby pretended to swoon. "His voice is an audio sex toy. One line and panties drop."

She laughed. "Then he'll fit in here just fine. You let me know if he is part of those fantasies of yours. I'm sure he'll be game for whatever you have in mind."

"Don't tease a girl like that."

She kissed Darby's cheek and whispered in her ear, "It's not a tease, but a promise."

"One I would be happy to fulfill. I've had my eye on the pixie since she arrived."

She smiled as she took her seat. Her telepathic connections grew stronger every day. This had been the first time she had used it to test out fantasy pairings. The gift had the potential of taking Taboo II even higher that she had ever imagined.

*

Jess patted his hand. "I need a moment to catch my second wind. I'll keep Mark company while you and Dani take a spin around the dance floor."

He raised her hand to his lips. "Don't go letting him sweep you off your feet while I'm gone. He's a charmer."

"She brings it out of me. How can I resist?" Mark draped his arm around her shoulders.

He stood and held his hand out to Danielle. "I think they're playing our song."

She tilted her head and took his hand as Aidan launched into the first notes of Dan Hill's "Sometimes When We Touch". He led her out to the center of the dance floor and brought her body close to his. In her heels she stood nearly tall enough to look him in the eyes. He had wanted to hold her this way all evening and had waited for the right moment. He had arranged with Aidan to sing this song for his dance with her. Words had never been his strong point, but with Mark he hadn't needed them. He wanted to show her how much she has come to mean to him and this song had always been one of his favorites.

"You have the best timing. I was about to steal you away from Jess. I've missed you all day."

She floated over the dance floor in his arms. Everyone else around them faded away except Aidan's soulful voice pouring out his heart through the words of the song. "I missed you, too. This is where I wish I had Mark's way with words. He would know exactly what to say. I get all tongue tied around you."

"You don't have to say anything. I feel what's in your heart. I *do* know you, Ian. Never doubt that or my love for you."

"I have no doubts, no more fears of never finding you and our place in the world. All of that fell away when you walked into the club. I've thanked the gods every single moment since then that Mark and I hopped on that plane to Elko."

"Babe, why are you shaking?" Her fingertips glided over his jawline.

"I love you. I don't know the exact moment when it happened, but…"

"It knocked you on your ass, didn't it?"

He laughed. "That's putting it mildly. It's been the two of us for so long. I never thought we would find another to complete our hearts the way you have. You're my world now. No matter who else may come or go, our family is complete."

The song ended as they swayed to the edge of the dance floor. He bent his head to bring his lips to hers. Her arms wrapped around his neck and her fingers combed through his hair, desperate to keep their connection. His tongue twirled around hers until one last barrier within him broke free.

"Where you go, I go. I will protect our family with my life."

*

Mark smiled. He knew Ian had struggled with allowing himself to be vulnerable and had encouraged him to open his heart and let it play out. It's what brought them together as kids and kept them together all these years. He alone knew Ian's rough and tough exterior hid his kind, caring soul. He counted himself as one of the luckiest men alive to be in love with both Ian and Danielle. Their love for each other would be the catalyst to get them through the months ahead.

Jess turned in her seat to see his face clearly. "You know, don't you?"

"Know what?" With all that faced them, he wasn't sure what she could be referring to now. He thought it best to keep it casual and let her volunteer the information.

"Don't be coy with me, love. Hok'ee and Fiona have withheld their identities from the three of you for far too long. It was only a matter of time before the truth came out, especially now that you'll be given the Gift of the Elders."

"Dani doesn't know about any of that yet. Fiona asked that we wait until she can tell us the entire story all at once."

Jess snorted. "I bet she did. She's always been the dramatic one. She and Hok'ee had been in love well before she ascended to Judge. Our mother had been in the position before her. It's always handed down to the first born of each generation. Ainthe would have been the choice if she had not given birth to Danielle and fulfilled the prophecy to the letter."

"What happened to Fiona's other Guardians?"

Her eyes widened and appeared to be stunned by his question. "There have always been three Guardians. One White…"

"One Black and one Gray."

"That's right. The night of the ascension, all your past memories will return. The two of you were not bound to Fiona but have always been Dani's fated mates. You've used the Gift of the Elders to come back in every lifetime until you found her again."

121

"How can that be?"

"How can a phoenix rise again? It's all magic and we're magical beings fighting for control over a great evil that's hell bent on destroying everything. If we don't win, Fitche will not only set Ouray ablaze, but the rest of the world with it."

He sat back in his chair and released the air he had held in his lungs while she spoke. "The Gift is as close to being an immortal as we can get. Once she ascends, will Dani be granted it as well?"

Jess nodded and smiled. "As White Witch she *is* the Gift in the flesh. You'll age slower than humans and they'll all want to know your secrets to keep looking so young. While the three of you can die, it's not forever. You will return, much like a phoenix."

His mind raced with the all the possibilities this ability would bring to the table. The advantages definitely outweighed the disadvantages. Over the coming days, he would be sure Fiona and Hok'ee brought them completely up to speed. He preferred to be prepared for any and all outcomes and have plans in place to protect Dani at all costs.

He looked up from the table as Ian returned her to the seat and took the seat next to him. The three of them clasped hands and energy zapped through them. Danielle's pupils dilated and he felt himself fall into the black pools.

We heard everything you and Jess talked about. This is how it should be. I'm not afraid of what we have to face. I have you, Ian, Black Wolf and Gray Wolf. Nothing else matters.

"Together we can get through anything. You've shown me that, Mark."

He gripped their hands and held them to his heart. It really didn't matter how they found each other or whether or not he and Ian had been Guardians before. Right here, right now was where they made their stand.

*

The party had gone on through the night and into the morning. Her cheeks hurt from smiling and laughing so much. She had introduced herself to hundreds of guests including celebrities who acted as if they had been friends forever. She didn't mind if it meant they're endorsement would help make Taboo a worldwide sensation. Her dream would be to open resorts in key locations all over the world, but for now she would be content with her little corner in Ouray.

By the time she had crawled into bed with Ian and Mark, her body had been running on pure adrenaline for at least five hours. As the last of it drained away, she'd been able to fall into a dreamless sleep. She had woken up still sandwiched between them five hours later. Somehow, she had managed to slip out of bed without disturbing them and raided the fridge for another yogurt parfait.

She sat down at the cherry wood desk and opened the Elder Grimoire. "Show me what to expect during the ascension."

The book opened and closed, the pages flipping rapidly in front of her eyes. With a thump the book dropped to the desk to the page she requested. She scanned through every word and paragraph, committing all of it to memory. The Wolf Clans would gather at dawn to form the Circle of Protection around Lake Lenore. The Elders from all Realms would walk with the White Witch and her Guardians to the alter set up in the middle of the lake. No mention on how they would travel to the alter, but she assumed it would be by a boat or canoe.

The rest of the details varied depending who would be present to represent each of the realms along with the Elders. With Seamus and Cael named as representatives of the Unseelie King, there would be no way to ban them from the ceremony as she had hoped. She wanted to save Aidan any additional pain a reunion with his brothers would cause. He had assured her there would be no way in hell he would miss being at her side. The best she could hope for was that the three brothers would be able to call a truce.

Mark appeared in the doorway to the kitchen, dressed in a pair of silk pajama bottoms. She would have preferred to see him naked, but with Rowan and Jess asleep in the guest bedrooms, it was probably best he had some clothing on. "Want me to put the kettle on?"

She shoved her reading glasses to the top of her head and smiled. "Yes, please." She got up from the chair and padded over the floor with in her fuzzy bunny slippers to join him in the kitchen. She slid her hands over his lower back and around to his abs. She rested her cheek against the middle of his back and hugged him tight.

"What got you up out of bed? I thought you wanted to sleep in this morning."

"It's after ten. I did sleep in"

"Not when we fell asleep at six." He reached his arm around to bring her to stand in front of him. "They don't expect us to show our faces downstairs until this afternoon."

"I wanted to study up on the ascension ceremony. It's a big deal in our world. Fitche hadn't objected when Fiona took over for her mother. It's *me* she objects to all the way around."

"Because you are more powerful than she could ever hope to be. You are the only one to stop her."

She shook her head. "There is one more." She pulled him out to the desk to show him what she had found in the Grimoire.

"Her father is Morpheus? That would make her a dragon shifter."

She nodded. "Morpheus fathered dozens of children with Lilith when she was Queen of all the Fae. The Courts weren't created until after she left the throne. Fitche feels she is the rightful heir to the throne as Lilith's daughter."

"As the original Dragon, he would be the one to destroy her and keep her from coming back. He's the one who forged the Fire Machete as the weapon to kill Angels, Dragons and a Phoenix."

"Why would he do that? What did he have against those beings?"

The book fluttered to life to answer her question. She hadn't intended to ask the book, if it had the answers they needed, then she would keep asking questions. The book fell open to a section near the front. Mark placed his finger next to the passage and read it aloud.

"The Gods asked their brother Morpheus to create a weapon to help rid them of any subject who threatened their rule or safety of the rest of the creations. He realized too late the Fire Machete would be used against him and his descendants for his betrayal of Lilith and Cane. To keep the weapon from falling into the wrong hands, Morpheus placed it in the safe keeping of one of The Fallen."

"Does it say how Fitche had it in her possession when she killed my father?"

He removed his finger from the page to see if it would find the answer for her. It remained still but emitted a high-pitched hum.

She jumped at the sound of a knock on their door. "Are you expecting anyone this morning?"

He shook his head. "Stay here. I'll get the door."

She rolled her eyes. "If it will make you feel better, then I'll stay put."

He mimicked her eye roll to perfection. "Don't be a smartass."

"But you love my ass."

He opened the door to find a stunning buxom blonde. "I'm quite fond of that ass myself."

"Siobhan!"

The Grimoire slammed shut. *"You have your answer, White Witch. Proceed with caution."*

Mark's eyes held hers, ready to slam the door in the woman's face. Danielle nodded. "What brings you to Colorado, and don't say it's my ass!"

She crossed the room in less than a dozen of her short strides. Siobhan bent to fold her into a bear hug. "I'm here to check out your new digs to see if I can convince my boyfriend to pull himself away from his latest project long enough for some one on one time."

Mark raised one of his eyebrows but held his tongue. She considered keeping him in the dark but thought better of it, especially after the way the Grimoire reacted to her. "I'm sorry to be so rude. Siobhan, this is one of my partners, Mark Zimmerman. Babe, this is Siobhan Walsh, actress and one of the Fallen.

"Damn, girl. You don't waste any time spilling my secret." She turned to Mark and held out her hand. "You must be one of her Guardians. Let me guess. You're Black Wolf."

He shook her hand and felt a mild jolt. He smiled. Danielle must have put up wards to protect him and Ian against any outsiders. "You're the one to give Fitche the machete."

Siobhan snapped her hand back from his grasp. "Not my finest moment, I assure you. That's why I'm here. I had hoped to be the one to tell you. I made a lot of mistakes since we were booted from Heaven. I'm trying to make amends now."

She opened her arm to direct her toward the living room while Mark grabbed Ian. She didn't want him to miss what the Angel had to say for herself. Not too long ago, she and Siobhan had one of the hottest whirlwind affairs of her life along with another of the Fallen. The two of them had taken her to heights of extasy she had only dreamed about until Mark and Ian entered her life.

Both men returned looking remarkably clear eyed and ready to take on the world. Their presence gave her the boost in confidence to pick up with the questions. "Unless you have an idea on how we can get the blade from Fitche, I'm not sure what you can do to help."

"I'm working on something at the moment. It involves my boyfriend's family. He's a Hawkins."

She held her hand up to stop her. "My aunt Jessalyn is asleep in our guest room. You'll be wise to not speak of that family while she is nearby."

Siobhan paled. "You're right. This can wait for another time. Let's say that I wish to lend my power to that of the Hawkins family. They are the representatives of the Human Realm here in Ouray. They may not know it yet, but they are and I can help concentrate their power when the time comes to face off with Fitche."

"They have to be here in Ouray to be of any help." Ian handed Siobhan a mug of coffee and one with tea to Danielle.

"My contacts in the Angel world tell me Jack's sister is headed back home soon. I don't know any details other than that. My guess is when she does decide to return, Jack will be with her and you'll have both of them here in eye of the storm."

She rested her elbow on the back of the couch and her head on her hand. "You've always been melodramatic, Von."

"Acting is a piece of cake compared to what all of us face if Ouray goes down. It's going to take the magic from all the Realms to come together to stop Fitche's minions."

"Do you know how we can reach Morpheus?" Mark sipped from his mug of coffee.

Siobhan shrugged. "I've sent out message after message throughout our usual contacts. Not one of them has been able to reach him. I don't know if he is deliberately ignoring me, or something is keeping him from receiving them."

"Why would he answer you?"

Anger flashed through her eyes and her nostrils flared. "What? You don't think Morpheus would stoop to fraternize with the likes of me?"

Mark lowered his mug to the coffee table. "That's not what I thought at all. If you have a bond, we may be able to amplify it to get him to hear you."

She closed her eyes and sunk into the cushions. "I'm sorry. I shouldn't have taken your head off like that. He…he's my father, too."

Danielle nearly choked on her tea. "How the hell is that possible?"

Siobhan smile didn't make it to her eyes. "Long before Lilith broke his heart, Morpheus had loved another goddess. I was the result of their forbidden union."

"I don't understand. Why was it forbidden?"

"They were siblings. Boann bore an eerie resemblance to Lilith. In his madness over losing her, Morpheus turned to his sister for comfort. Unable to deny him anything, she gave herself to him freely. After his banishment, Boann went on to have her child."

"She couldn't bear the constant reminder of a love she couldn't have so I ended up at the mercy of Heaven."

Danielle sensed Siobhan's overwhelming sadness and shame, something no child should ever have to feel. "You are your own being now and are not responsible for the mistakes or your parents. For what it's worth, we accept your offer to help as long as all parties are receptive to it."

The color returned to the Angel's cheeks. "Thank you. I'll do my best to come through for you and Ouray. Now, if I'm not mistaken the sound of the shower running means that Jessalyn has awakened. I'll leave all of you to your busy schedule. I'd like to check in with Aidan before I head back out to the airport."

Ian got up to see her out and joined them back on the sofa. "I don't know about the rest of you, but I'm getting a wee bit lost with the connections between everyone. Rowan, are you sure Mark and I aren't Dani's long-lost brothers?"

The witch laughed until tears rolled down her cheeks. "You're not nor have you ever been connected by blood. You're three pieces of the same heart and soul. Remember that when Fitche tosses her garbage out at you, and she will."

"Were the lot of you going to let me sleep the day away? I have to get back to the ranch. The place doesn't run itself you know."

"You know damn well they have things covered for the weekend. You and I are moving out to their farmhouse to be closer to the lake. We have to prepare for next week and welcome the Elders."

Mark hid his smile behind his coffee mug. He appeared to be thoroughly enjoying the sisterly banter.

Ian did his best to appear to be crushed they were leaving them. "I give you the night to remember and you were going to leave without so much as a word?"

Jess pulled her glasses down her nose to glare at him. "I would think you would be too worn out after last night. I seem to recall someone crying uncle well before last call."

He bowed before her. "Have mercy. You're too much of a woman for the likes of me."

"Damn straight. Now get your foolish ass up off the floor and give me some sugar."

He lifted her off her feet and spun her around. Her laughter filled the room. These are the times Danielle would treasure the most—fun, spontaneous, and filled with laughter.

Those will be their way to defeat the soulless Fetche.

Chapter 12

The Elders gathered together in the caverns beneath Lake Lenore, the body of water sacred to all magical realms. No blood had ever been shed there, even in the most tumultuous times and all present pledged to keep it that way.

Shaman Hok'ee stood before them and brought their meeting to order. "We've gathered here once again to reaffirm our pledge to bring any and all grievances between us to be heard by the Judge of the Realms and prepare for the transfer of power to the new Judge and her Guardians. As always, representatives of each Realm have the right to speak before the Elders and express any objections they have before the ascension takes place."

Fiona stood next to him and scanned all those seated before her. "It had been agreed from the very beginning that until the one foretold by the Prophesy came into her own, The Elders would appoint the first born of every generation of Witches to serve as Judge. My time as Judge is nearing its end."

Seamus the Blue Phoenix stood. "Who shall take your place, Purple Witch? Correct me if I'm wrong, but there isn't another of your clan powerful enough to take your place."

Aidan stepped into view. "I see you're still playing the fool, brother."

Seamus stared at him with disbelief. "Why were we not told you were alive?"

Aidan laughed. "You mean, why weren't you given a head's up I would already be here protecting the White Witch from you?"

The Seelie King stood. "We know of the bad blood between the three of you. There will be time to present your case before the Judge after the ascension. Fiona, with all due respect, please answer

Seamus's question so all will have confirmation she has come back into her power."

Cael reached for his brother and stopped him from lunging at Aidan. "If you're referring to a child the Witches claim is the daughter of Aithne and Phalen, we ask for proof. If she is indeed the White Witch, the Unseelie King will support her ascension without question."

Danielle stepped forward, flanked by Ian and Mark. Shaman placed a bowl on the altar next to the black pearl handled athame. She picked up the blade and drew it across the palm of her left hand. She created a fist to force the blood to stream into the bowl. Fiona chanted as she dropped herbs into the bowl. Danielle used the tip of the dagger to mix the contents and added her voice to the spell.

"Blood of Witch, Fae, Human and Shifter combined with the Angel fulfill the prophecy. I stand before you as descendent of all, White Witch, and Heir to the Realms. So mote it be."

The contents in the bowl burst into white flame, traveled up her arm and covered her body. There she stood in front of them all, completely engulfed in the phoenix fire and not even breaking a sweat.

"This is so cool. Aidan, why didn't you tell me this would happen?"
"Would you believe me if I did?"
"Focus, dear. We'll have time to discuss the details later. They're about to put it to a vote."

Seamus and Cael's eyes filled with wonder. "It's true. White Witch has been reborn." Both dropped to there knees and bowed before her.

All the other representatives followed suit, including the Seelie King. He took her hand, unafraid of the flame. "We've waited so long. Welcome home, Danielle. We welcome your rule as Judge of the Realms."

Jess stood. "As the representative of the Human Realm as well as Witch we move to complete the transfer of power and the ascension of White Witch here and now."

Shaman raised his hands. "What say you, all?"

"Aye!"

Her body elevated and floated to the center of the room. The white flames swirled around her, lifting her above their heads. Her eyes darted toward Aidan to be sure this is what was supposed to happen when the flames lifted her. Her heartbeat quickened at the sight of his smile. She reached out to Ian and Mark Their eyes never left hers as the white flame elevated them up to her. Her fingers entwined with theirs and the flames intensified.

"What do you say, White Witch? Do you accept the mantle as Judge and Protector of the Realms?"

Momentarily taken aback by Shaman's use of her new title, she held her tongue. She looked to all the faces in the cavern turned up toward her. All appeared happy and eager for her to accept. She smiled and squeezed Ian and Mark's hands.

"Aye!"

Ian and Mark wrapped their arms around her as Aidan had instructed them to do. They brought their breathing and heart beats in sync. With each breath and beat, the floated to the floor and the flame dimmed. The moment their feet planted on the cavern floor, the fire extinguished. Her knees buckled as the energy dispersed from her body.

"We have you, darlin'."
"Almost over now. You did it, honey."

She stood before them all once again and greeted each Elder and representative by name. Seamus and Cael stayed behind in hopes to speak with her. In her mind she saw them stand by while her father had been ripped apart, but now something changed. This time she connected with their memories of that day. They stood before her now, their heads bowed with shame.

Cael found his voice first. "One day we hope to earn your trust. Until then, know we will do whatever is within our power to keep you safe from Fitche. She has destroyed all that had been good in our lives." His eyes looked toward Aidan.

"You have every right to punish us for our part in Phalen's death."

She held out her hands to each of them. "You relive that day over and over in your mind, asleep or awake. That is punishment enough. Go in peace. But know this. As with the Wolf Clans who chose the Darkness over the Light, if we find you have continued to betray us, your life will be forfeit. Please don't make me regret putting my faith in you."

They placed their other hands over their hearts and swore to protect her and her Guardians. "We must return to our king and give him the news. He will be most pleased."

She smiled. "Pleased for himself, or that it will piss off Fitche?"

Her uncles laughed. Seamus shook hands with both Ian and Mark. "King Brennus takes great pleasure in riling her up and watching her explode."

"That seems dangerous even for him." Aidan chimed into the conversation but still kept his distance from his brothers.

Cael nodded. "Aye. That's another reason why we're here. We don't think Brennus will be able to control her for much longer. She's gathering her supporters as we speak, including her half-breeds."

"Duly noted. Send our regards to King Brennus. Any enemy of Fitche has safe passage here." She stepped back to allow them to move out of the caverns and pass through the Circle of Protection.

Fiona's hand brushed her shoulder. "How do you feel, dear heart?"

She smiled and swayed. "I could sleep for a week. Flaming out is exhausting."

Aidan kissed her cheek. "The more you use your power, the less it drains you. For now, you need to rest, Judge and Protector of the Realms."

"Stop it. You can still call me your Little Lynx."

"Whew! I was going to say that we need to shorten your title to something that rolls off the tongue. Give me a day or two and I'll have something."

"Deal."

As they walked through the passages back to the opening hidden within the stone bridge that connected the Brooks' estate to their property, the enormity of what occurred hit her. No more will she have to wonder where she came from or if she was some freak of nature. She had finally found her way back to her home and her rightful place in the world.

Now the real work would begin.

Fiona and Hok'ee agreed to stay with them at the farmhouse. The hustle and bustle of the resort had proved to be more than the older couple could handle for more than a few hours at a time. Danielle didn't blame them. While she loved the chaos, she found the quiet time home in the house more to her liking. There she could show off her culinary skills in wow their guests with anything from simple barbecue to full five-course meal.

Ian and Hok'ee argued over the best way to build a fire in the fireplace, while Mark looked on. He refused to take sides in the matter. "Why don't you combine your methods? Seems to me that would create the best outcome and we could be enjoying the heat by now."

Fiona laughed. "It's good to see Hok'ee relax."

"He has been rather intense. I assumed he chilled more because of you."

"We do have that effect on each other, much like Ian and Mark have with you. It makes me happy to see they've finally found their place."

She stopped chopping the onions on the cutting board. "So, it's true? They were once your Guardians?"

Fiona sighed. "It's not that simple. In one lifetime, Black and Gray Wolf agreed to join with White Wolf and I. Hok'ee and I were lovers. The other two were content to protect us but I didn't feel right about keeping them from finding their soulmate. Even then I knew the two of them were destined to be with one woman. Their bond wouldn't allow anything else."

"The night they showed up in my club in Elko, I knew I was a goner."

"That's the best kind, isn't it? The all-consuming passion between the three of you is palpable to all around you. I know your life with Eileen wasn't easy, but I saw no other way to protect you. Fitche has spies everywhere in the Realms. Eileen had given up all claims to her magic and fell off their radar."

"There is no point in reliving all of that. Unless it's a memory or vision that will help us with the fight we have ahead of us, I don't want to rehash any of it, if that's okay with you."

"Agreed. You've made a damn good life for yourself here already. It's good to see you so happy."

"I could same the same for you with Hok'ee. Will the two of you settle here or travel the world?" She tossed the onions into a skillet to sauté while she chopped up several cloves of fresh garlic.

"We'll stay as long as Fitche is on the loose. We've been in hiding long enough. Battle lines will need to be drawn. Here is where we make our stand. Many lives will be lost in this as her wrath burns through the land."

"Wildfires are the perfect cover for her plans. Have enough of them converge on Ouray and she'll have us right where she wants us."

"As always, Jessalyn is busy organizing supplies and coordinating evacuation plans. She's been doing this for decades here. Tap into her expertise. She'll need you close by when her Callista falls to her depression."

"Wait. Isn't Callista Hawkins the Guardian Healer of the Arrow?"

"She has not accepted her destiny yet. Up until six years ago, her grandfather Jonah served in her place. Now he's gone as well as Theresa Brooks. Callista must return home soon to help keep Ouray out of Fitche's grasp."

Her mind filed away the new information to use later. For now, her hands were full with Taboo and fitting in with the small-town life in Ouray. So far, they've encountered a few residents who condemn their lifestyle. They see nothing wrong with stumbling out of the bars at all hours, or idiots trespassing and poaching, but offer a safe place for consenting adults to explore their sexual fantasies and you're immediately placed on the perv list.

Fuck them. She refused to stoop to their level. Instead she would make Taboo a vital part of the town evacuation plans. That alone would win most of the naysayers over. At one time in her life she had thought humans had the potential of being the cruelest creatures on earth. She still ranked them up there, right next to good old Grandma Fitche. She suppressed a smile thinking of how that title would piss the broad off even further.

For shits and giggles, she had looked up the meaning of the Unseelie Queen's name. She must have been one ugly baby for her mother to give her a name that means ermine. Slapping a kid with the name Apple was bad enough, but to saddle your daughter with a name describing her as a weasel had to be the worst. From all the stories she had heard about Lilith, there had to be another reason she branded one of her children this way.

Chapter 13

Danielle threw the car into park and grabbed her bag from the passenger seat. Jess had called her unable to speak between her sobs. Without another question she had told her aunt she would drive out to the Hawkins Ranch to see her in person.

She ran up the porch steps and grabbed the handle of the screen door. "Jess! Where are you?"

She heard the kitchen chair scrape against the floor followed by fast moving footsteps. "Dani?"

Her heart fell to see Jess's tear streaked face. No one would make her cry like that except for the children she had raised as her own. She held the older woman as her body shook with fresh tears. "What the hell happened?"

"Callie tried to kill herself."

"What? That can't be right."

"Jack said they found her unconscious on the floor of her office."

Danielle had been keeping tabs the young Doctor Hawkins ever since Zachary had confessed he had fallen in love with the woman. This news would devastate him as well. She assumed Callista had given everything she had to her career in order to become board certified in wildlife and emergency medicine. As one of the top veterinary criticalists in the country, she must be swamped with patients all of the time. Anyone would break under that kind of pressure.

"Sit down on the couch and tell me everything you can remember from your conversation with Jack." She grabbed the box of Kleenex from the end table and handed it to her.

Jess blew her nose and dabbed her eyes. "He said, she's been in the hospital for the last four days. He didn't want to call me until she woke up. I knew something was wrong with her. I could feel it in my bones."

She held Jess's hands in hers. "Think about her now. Maybe I can connect with her and we'll get more of the story." She closed her eyes and slowed her breathing. She reached out through Jess's mind. Their magic joined together to travel to the hospital where Callista lay asleep in the hospital bed. Together they eased into her mind and relived the horrors of the last hours before she swallowed the bottle of oxycodone. Tears ran down her cheeks as she experienced the grief and overwhelming sense of failure that had ripped Callista's heart apart leaving nothing left for herself.

Danielle sent healing light and love to the beautiful woman.

"Come home, Callie. Ouray needs you."

She brought Jess back with her. "She's going to get through this. She has Jack and you. Let's not forget Zach."

"He was about to jump in his truck to drive all the way to Seattle to sit by her bedside until I told him it would be of no use. They would only allow Jack to be in there with her. Besides, Jack said they'll release her tomorrow and to expect them within the week."

"There you go. She'll be here before you know it. If she is anything like you and Zach have told me, then you know she'll jump right in to help out with the sanctuary."

"They really could use her expertise. Don Caron hasn't a clue how to run that place let alone evacuate the animals. He hasn't even started a plan yet. If Jonah were alive, no way in hell would he wait this long to have his plan in place."

"You let me worry about that. I have some connections I can tap into to give the volunteers a had to move the animals out. In the meantime, it will be a good idea to keep Zach busy. Why don't you create one of your famous lists on your notepad? Make sure you have him deliver more supplies up to our storage barns. We're set to be the evac headquarters and our land is open to set up the evac camps like you all did last year."

"I can't help feeling this is one more thing Fitche is trying to use to break out spirits. If I find out she had anything to do with Callie trying to harm herself…"

"She will pay dearly for every infraction. This I swear to you. Let me worry about Fitche. You do what you do best here at the ranch."

Jess threw her arms around her. "Thank you for rushing out here to check on me. I don't know what I would have done without you. Rowan went with Fiona and Hok'ee to pick up his granddaughter in Denver."

"Aidan doesn't know she's on her way. We thought it best to not get his hopes up for a happy reunion. Hok'ee has been pretty tight-lipped about the whole thing."

Jess smiled. "More sparks will fly between those two before it's over, that I can tell you."

"I thought we agreed there would be no more riddles."

"Old habits. Now go on. Get back to that farmhouse. Spend time with the stud muffins before you're overrun with guests again."

"Full house or not, we manage to get in our alone time, thank you very much."

Jess chuckled. "I bet you do."

*

"What did you think of her?" She sat across from Mark at their kitchen table.

"Callie? She's a smartass like Jess. I love her already."

"Now I can't wait to meet her myself. Did you say she was going to scout out properties this direction for evac camps?"

"That was there plan when Jess and I left for the meeting with Lester. I was happy to see him tell that hot head Berringer to suck it. You and Jess can handle the evacuation headquarters better without any interference from the town council."

"Zach and Chuck each made four deliveries of supplies today. The residents and businesses are really banding together. The Wolf Clans are organizing relief and evacuation efforts in Durango and Silverton. Lester agrees with our plan to have everything in place and ready to roll before we're under mandatory evacuation."

She peered out the window to see a golf cart traveling at high speed over the low grassy hills of the property adjacent to theirs. "That wouldn't be them now, would it?"

Mark joined her at the window and laughed. "Yes, it is. I can hear her laughter from here. Why don't you go on over and introduce yourself and get a feel for how she's doing?"

"You picked up on her darkness, didn't you?"

He shrugged. "A glimmer of it. She is scared she's going to fail and let everyone down."

"She shouldn't have so much weight on her shoulders when there are those who will help take on part of the burden."

He rubbed his thumb over her chin. "You're one to talk, sweetheart."

She tilted her face toward his. "I don't always have a choice as an empath, but I'm learning how to channel it to share with you and Ian so I'm not overwhelmed. I don't need a repeat performance like what happened with Aidan."

"That's different. You saw the murder of your father through Aidan's eyes. There's no way to disconnect from your emotions with that one. As for the others, keep our connection open and we'll help you through."

He bent to kiss her. His lips brushed over hers and sent the butterflies dancing in her stomach. With a kiss alone, Mark turned her mind to mush. He chuckled at how she had to hold on to him until her legs stopped wobbling. "You do the same for me every single time. Now go before I flip you over my shoulder and toss you on our bed."

She twisted out of his arms and blew him a kiss. "I won't be long. I expect to pick up where we left off when I get back."

"Count on it."

Danielle picked up her keys from the small table near the door and hopped into her red Mustang. With the way Jack careened over the property in the golf cart, she had very little chance to catch up with them on foot. She drove the short distance from her driveway to the entrance of the Brooks' estate. The long, winding drive toward the main house gave her a moment to clear her mind of all other thoughts and concentrate on Callista.

She parked next to their jeep and stood out in front of both vehicles waving her arms to get their attention. It appeared to work as the golf cart suddenly took off again at top speed, Callista's squeals of laughter reached her ears.

The cart lurched to a stop in front of her, creating a light cloud of dust. A sharp pang of jealousy passed through her in an instant. She envied their sibling bond and wished she had someone to lean on when she was growing up. She felt the same way whenever she witnessed Jess and Rowan's ribbing.

"That looked like fun. You wouldn't happen to be Jack and Callista would you?"

He removed his sunglasses and held out his hand. "In the flesh. You must be Danielle from Taboo."

Callista narrowed her eyes. "How did you know that?"

He pointed to his head. "Jess said she had pink and purple hair. Who else could it be?"

Danielle laughed again. "Guilty! Jess and I are working together on the evacuation committee. I saw the jeep and took a chance it was you."

"I had hoped to meet you today. We had breakfast with Mark this morning but I wanted to thank you in person for volunteering your property for the evac camp."

"It's the least we could do. Ouray is our home."

"Exactly. That's why I'm making an offer on this place. It's perfect to add to yours for the camp."

"And for your forever home?"

Jack and Callista exchanged looks. "You think?"

"What?" She kept her expression neutral. Times like these she found it best to not to admit right off you can read their thoughts and emotions.

Jack jumped right in. "I'm not going to wait years this time. Are you like Jess, a witch?"

Callista slapped his arm. "You can't go around asking people you meet if they're a witch."

Danielle smiled and her eyes twinkled. "Why not? Ouray is full of magical beings "Seriously?" Callista's eyes filled with excitement.

"I knew it!"

"Jack! I think you've had enough fun for one day. Can you store this thing??

He waved and pulled away from them. Thankfully he didn't kick up a bunch of dust this time.

"He's a dork but he has a heart of gold."

Danielle took her hands. "No worries. I've wanted to meet you as soon as I heard you came back. Zach talked about you all the time. Anyone who can make him smile is a friend of ours." She thought it best not to discuss their family ties until Jess gave her the okay.

"Oh? Is he a regular at Taboo?"

"He stops in from time to time to hang out with Ian and Mark. Don't worry. His heart has always belonged to you."

Her cheeks turned a flattering shade of pink. "Good to know."

Danielle took her other hands and her mind filled with images running by at warp speed. She would sort all of it out later, but for now she had the chance to answer put some of Callista's doubts to rest. "I know you have a lot of questions, but how about we table those for another time. I can tell you about this property. Miss Brooks held on to it for you."

"Me? I don't understand."

"The magic here needs balance. No one but the descendants of the original Guardians could possess this land. There were two clans given the honor. One was the Brooks family and the other is yours."

"This is your legacy, Callie girl. Hold on and don't let go."
"I hear you, Gramps!"

Danielle overheard their exchange and smiled. "He will help you on your new path, Callie girl. Trust what your heart tells you and above all else, believe in miracles."

"Thank you for that." Callista hugged her and joined her brother waiting for her in the Jeep.

She waved as they drove down the driveway. She could see why Zachary fell in love with her. Callista's spirit called out to her, too. This was one woman born to lead. She had no doubt the evac of the sanctuary would proceed with or without Caron's help. If he proved true to form, Callista would have no choice other than fire his ass. She hoped it wouldn't come to that. It could be the catalyst to finally push him over the edge.

Their encounters at the sanctuary had been brief and he had yet to attend any town council meeting since Mark took his post in late January. It's as if he is deliberately separating himself from his connections in Ouray. That may make a lot of the residents happy, but it sent warning bells off in her head. Ian's idea that Caron could very well be under the influence of Fitche, seemed more probable than not. His erratic behavior concerning her property and what will now belong to Callista confirmed it for her.

She turned her attention south toward town. The smoky haze she had grown accustomed to since the end of April had taken on an otherworldly appearance. The mountains appeared to change colors from yellow to orange and back again. Her stomach dropped. Fitche's dragons had been busy overnight fanning the flames of the fires already out of control.

"Fuck me."

She slid behind the wheel and sped down the driveway back home. The time had come to send out the calls for help. Ouray needed all the magic she could muster to make their stand against the Unseelie Queen.

She smiled as she pulled up to the detached garage to find Aidan's motorcycle parked inside as well as Shaman's Hummer. Aidan and Rain must have kissed and made up for him to be at the house the same time as the Sandovals. The sound of Rain's laughter confirmed her suspicion.

"Siobhan is stuck on location for another week but promises to be here as soon as she can break free." She tossed her phone down on the table and combed her fingers through her hair. She would be in need of a cut soon. The thought of it brought up images of Faye. With the wildfires converging, Danielle thought it best Tony kept Faye and Lia safe in Elko. No need to put their lives at risk. She had too much going on now to worry about them on top of it.

Rain's dark eyes bore into hers. "Almost half of the Healers have already arrived. They're working with The Sisters to create a spell strong enough to protect Ouray. We will need someone from all the Realms to focus the magic."

She agreed. "That's coming together as we speak. Callista Hawkins has returned and appears to be accepting her destiny as Guardian. Her brother has volunteered to fly the helicopters with Fire and Rescue.

Mark's phone chimed. He grinned as he read the message. "Callista has called meeting for tomorrow morning at the sanctuary to go over the evacuation plans. She doesn't waste time."

She glanced at her own phone as she received the same message. "No, she doesn't and it's exactly what this town needs to remind them of the danger we're facing. Once they see the Hawkins family taking the lead and being proactive with the evacuations, they'll be ready to roll faster when the folks from Durango and Silverton make their way here for shelter."

"I'll go with you to the volunteer meeting. I'd like to see what bullshit Caron will try to pull to get out of this one."

"Hok'ee and I will be at Hawkins Ranch helping the fire crews get settled in. Jess is a dynamo but even she can't take care of all of this on her own." Mark pulled out a yellow note pad and jotted down additional notes.

Danielle grinned. "I see you've picked up another of her habits, babe."

He waved the pad in the air. "Electronics get old and batteries die. Give me a pen and paper and I'm ready to rock and roll."

Fiona laughed. "Don't go telling my sister about the notepads. We'll never hear the end of it. I'll meet the next wave of Healers at the airport in the morning. That will free up Rain to work with Aidan. Your fire dance will have to be perfect to make the rest of the spell go off without a hitch."

Rain bit her lip as Aidan reached for her hand under the table. "We'll be ready when the time comes."

"I'd say that's enough for tonight. We'll check in again after the meeting at the sanctuary." She stood and hugged their guests as she bid them goodnight. She stripped out of her clothes and tossed them into the hamper. She stepped into the shower and closed her eyes as the water cascaded over her head and down her back. The doors slid open and Ian's mouth sealed over her left nipple. She moaned and held his head to her breast, urging him to suck harder. He released her nipple with a loud pop and snaked his tongue between her tits, up her neck and to her mouth.

His hand slid down her stomach and between her thighs. He slid one finger into her as his mouth devoured hers. She moaned as he fucked her with his fingers, his thumb rhythmically strumming her clit. Her body hummed with need and desire to be taken right then and there but she knew better. Ian had plans for her that didn't include a shower time quickie. No, he would tease and tease until she begged for mercy and do it all again.

Exactly the way she liked it.

He lifted her in his arms and sat down on the bench in the shower. The steady stream of water and steam covered their bodies, keeping them slick and slippery. He parted her legs and slid the head of his cock through her outer lips, over her clit and back again. Eyes wide open to deepen their connection as he pushed into her.

She bit his lower lip as he lowered her down over his shaft, burying himself in her spasming pussy. The pleasure and pain melted into one and her body convulsed. A rush of warmth shot out of her and was his signal to move her. He dug his fingers into her ass and gave into her need to take over the pace. She bounced up and down, tilted her hips forward and back and in circles to hit every hot zone within her.

She clung to him as he thrust into her faster and harder. No more teasing. No more playing. Just raw animalistic need.

"Dani…" He groaned her name against her neck as she collapsed against him. Her body quaked as the last orgasm flew through both of them.

The water had lost some of its heat, but she didn't care. The fire between them kept her warm. She wanted more. More of him. Mark. The three of them together at once.

"He's waiting for us." He nipped her ear and rubbed his stubble along her neck.

The way he knew would render her putty in his hands.

He reached for the soap and lathered her body paying close attention to her ass and pussy. She ran the scrunchy and her soapy hands over every inch of him as well. His cock came to life again at her touch as the water rinsed away the last of the soap.

He stepped out first and wrapped one of the towels around his waist. He held out his hand to help her from the stall. She attempted to dry herself off, but he snatched the towel from her. "Let me take care of you, darlin'."

She stood in front of him, her back to his chest as he moved the soft cloth over her curves and through her hair. When satisfied with his work, he picked her up and carried her back to their bedroom. As promised, Mark lay naked in the center, his cock eagerly awaiting her arrival.

He smiled and rolled a condom over his dick and coated it with their favorite anal lube.

Her pussy clenched over and over as another rush of fluid trickled out of her. Ian helped her up onto the bed to straddle Mark's hips. His fingers worked the lube into her ass, stretching and strumming the inner muscle rings. She gasped as the head of Mark's cock eased into her tight hole. He pulled her body against his and spread her legs.

Ian licked his lips at the sight of Mark's cock buried in her ass. He moved between both of their legs and positioned his cock at the entrance of her cunt. "Are you, ready to take both of us, darlin'?"

She nodded and reached for him, trusting Mark to keep her in position. Ian kissed her and thrust his tongue into her mouth as his cock slammed home. She moved her legs up to hook over his hips as he moved in and out of her. Mark timed his movements to be in sync with Ian, filling her completely. Wave after wave of ecstasy flowed through the three of them. Danielle's body opened to both of her lovers and still demanded more.

Her vision blurred as brilliant light exploded in her mind and slowly faded to black.

She awoke seconds later, the three of them on their sides, arms and legs entangled with each other. She sighed. Content and satiated for the moment. She knew her body well. It wouldn't be long before the cravings hit again.

Mark kissed her neck and shoulder. "You okay, sweetheart?"

"Mmmhmm." She moved her left hand up to rest against his cheek.

Ian slid his hand over her thigh. "You know we can't stay like this for much longer. You won't be able to walk."

She snorted. "Walking is overrated."

Her men chuckled. She loved the sound especially when they lay together like this. Their laughter rumbled in their chests and tickled her body between them. Moments like this had been all she'd ever wanted. Now she had it and no one would take it away from her. Her heart belonged to both of them. The three of them wouldn't exist without the other.

She whimpered as each of their cocks softened and slipped out of her. While her lustful cravings for them had been temporarily satisfied, her desire to continue to touch and taste never abated. She had wondered if it would always be this way between them and received her answer the moment she witnessed Hok'ee and Fiona together.

Her eyelids grew heavy but she struggled to stay awake, to commit this moment to memory.

"Go to sleep, darlin'. We're not going anywhere."

"Let your mind rest, sweetheart."

"I love you…"

"We love you, too. Sleep now for tomorrow we draw the line in the sand."

Chapter 14

Danielle stood at the door along with Ian waiting for Callista and Zachary to arrive. "There they are. Can't miss Gunnar. I've never seen a support dog as social as he is."

Ian laughed. "He is a charmer that's for sure. Zach said Gunnar may appear to be distracted, but he can pick up on his anxiety even before he knows he's having any problems."

"I'm happy the VA was finally able to swing it. Both Callie and Zach need Gunnar in their lives. He picked Zach for a reason."

"You've seen Jonah around haven't you?"

"Maybe. He's not the only ghost hanging around Ouray to protect their family. Besides, he is a Hawkins. They take their oath as Guardian seriously."

"Are you implying I don't?" He winked and hugged her.

"Oh you! Of course not. Humans are a different lot when it comes to being Guardians."

The couple they had been watching finally made it to the door through all the volunteers. "Z-man!"

Zachary shook Ian's hand. "Good to see you both here. Callie, this is Ian Campbell. You've already met Dani."

Danielle hugged her and whispered in her ear, "Open your heart. Everyone will follow your lead."

Ian shook her hand and smiled. "We wanted to be here to show our support. Mark will meet up with all of us later. He wanted me to be sure to tell you to kick ass."

"With all of your support, I think I might be able to pull it off." She awarded Ian with a smile that would have knocked him off his feet if he hadn't already been leaning against the door.

Callista took Zachary's hand as they followed the crowd into the auditorium in the main building. She left him and Zachary at their seats as she headed up the steps to the stage.

"I told you she was a knockout." Danielle slipped her hand into his as they settled into their seats.

"That she is. If Zach wasn't in the picture…"

"The thought had crossed my mind too. She would make a wonderful addition to our family."

"Still could, but not in the bedroom." He glanced toward her to gauge her reaction and was happy to see she agreed.

Callista paused momentarily as she crossed the stage to the podium. Ian glanced in the direction she had been looking to find Don Caron's scowling face. He prepared to launch at the stage if the jackass tried anything. He turned to check out the audience and had been surprised to see so many other folks from the magical realms there along with the human residents of Ouray. Looked like the rumors he heard were true. There has always been a Hawkins in the middle of rallying the town into action.

She cleared her throat and waited while her audience settled into their seats. Her eyes sought out Zachary and Gunnar and she visibly stood taller. "Good Morning. I want to thank all of you for starting your day off so early to join me here. I see a few familiar faces but most of you don't know me from Adam. My name is Callista Hawkins and I'm here today to outline the evacuation and relocation of the sanctuary residents."

"It's about time."

She smiled and looked in the direction of the voice. "I agree. I toured the facility last night and witnessed first-hand how hard all of you have worked to care for our charges. You promised to protect them from harm and as such we have to act now. The fires are closer than they've ever been to us at this time of year. We can't afford to lose any more time."

"Excuse me, *Doctor* Hawkins, but what makes you qualified to make that decision? I have a letter from the fire chief."

"That says what? The evac of the sanctuary will get in the way of the fire crews? Save it. I talked to Frank on the way over here. As for my qualifications, anyone can find them online but if it will ease your mind…" The screen behind her came to life with a slide detailing her credentials, board certifications and state license information.

She clicked the button to advance to the next slide showing a split screen with her credentials next to Don's. A swirl of loud murmurs and shouted questions indicated their emotions were running high. She held up her hands asking them for calm.

"Slam dunk. Callie knows how to handle this prick."

Danielle agreed. "He's no match for her and he knows it."

"I'm not here to embarrass anyone, but I won't sit by and have my qualifications and intentions questioned. I'm asking for help. You can either join me or get the hell out of my way."

The crowd erupted into applause and cheers.

"Now we're talking!"

"Kick him to the curb, Callie!"

Gunnar barked his approval.

Danielle held both of her fists in the air and encouraged her to keep rolling. "She's on fire now."

"Agreed."

"Ouray's a small town so I'm sure most, if not all of you have heard by now that I've purchased the Brooks estate north of town between Taboo and Lake Lenore. With the two properties combined, we now have enough room for the evac camps and a safe haven for the sanctuary residents."

"Over my dead body. That property was supposed to be mine. My offer was on the table long before you came back here."

She sighed. "The executor of Theresa Brooks' estate accepted my offer. I was told all other offers on the property had been refused by Ms. Brooks before her death."

"There you go again, throwing your name and money around. It's taken me years to be in the position to be able to buy back my family land, and in one day you've taken that away."

"This man has officially gone off the deep end. He knows his claims aren't legit and he keeps up the ruse. What the hell is wrong with him?"

"Has to be a connection with Fitche. He is irrational when it comes to our properties."

Callista's eyes scanned the audience, looking for someone who could help her calm him down. "I'm sorry, Mr. Caron. The sale is final. All the paperwork has been signed and filed with the proper agencies.

"The town council assured me the sale to *me* would go through." Don's face turned bright purple.

Ian had enough and stood with his arms crossed over his chest. "And this happened when? My partner, Mark Zimmerman has been on that council since Taboo opened in January and you've been MIA. Care to explain that?"

Don narrowed his eyes. "You and your kind are what's wrong with this town."

Several others stood up with Ian, some shifters and other non-humans daring Don to say one more word. Callista turned toward him to give him one last chance. "Please. Can we count on you to help with the evac?"

He snorted in disgust and stormed off the stage.

"Okay then. How about we get back to the business at hand."

The next two hours seemed to fly by. She held their attention through every minute as she detailed her plan. Each compound coordinator and the staff veterinarians had received copies specific to their teams. Their first priority that afternoon would be the birds of prey as they were the most sensitive to the smoke and fires. Additional groups volunteered to start moving the feed and other supplies needed out to the new storage areas. Zachary, Chuck and a dozen others broke off into their own group to discuss building the additional shelf space and conversion of one of the barns into the orphan ward.

Ian smiled and squeezed Danielle's hand. "This is how mountain people take care of their own. They come together and put aside their differences to keep everyone safe. Caron would be wise to remember that."

"He claims to have ties here, but I have yet to see any evidence of it. From what I've heard, he has separated himself from everyone from the moment he arrived. We need to figure out what is controlling him and send them packing. Ouray doesn't need him mucking up what we have going on now."

They stood and headed for the exit. He turned to get one more look at Callista in action. She held court with the staff of the veterinary hospital. All of them appeared to be happy someone had heard their concerns and were making the changes needed to protect the animals. "I'd like to head over to Callista's place and if we can lend some extra help to get the new shelters ready for the sanctuary residents. I'm thinking Hok'ee would want to be involved as much as possible, especially with the eagles, Elvis and Priscilla. He's been visiting their current digs almost daily."

"Good idea. Now that the sanctuary evac plan is underway, Jess and I will have to step up our game with setting up the evac headquarters at Taboo. I'd like to set up another set of service reps along the windows to the left of the main front desk. This way there will be no confusion for evacuees when they check in."

He dropped his arm over her shoulders as her arm slid around his waist. "I have to admit, I have had my doubts the humans would get their shit together to pull this off. Callista has opened my eyes."

"I had to trust in the magic of Ouray to wake them up and bring the rest of its Guardians home. With Jack and Callista here, our circle is complete. Of course, we could always add more, like Siobhan with the Hawkins family. Aidan will assist Rain, and we'll have three of the Four Sisters. If anymore of my family happen to show up we'll put them to good use!"

*

They made it through the throng of tourists on Main Street when her phone rang. The Caller ID told her the call was from Zachary. With Ian at the wheel, she answered her phone without having to have it connected to the car. "What's up, Zach?"

"It's Callista. Sorry for the confusion. I found your number on his phone."

The other woman's emotions filled her mind but she couldn't pinpoint what had her so upset. "Do you need us to turn around?"

"No, no. We have it under control now. Gunnar was attacked by a swarm of wasps outside the sanctuary as we were leaving."

Then it clicked. Callista opened her mind and Danielle saw every moment play out in slow motion. This had to be how it seemed to the other woman with her training and expertise. It still freaked the shit out of Danielle to witness it. "Is Gunnar going to make it?" Her vision blurred with tears.

Ian snapped his eyes away from the road. His face registering her fear their friend had lost his companion. He grabbed her hand and held on waiting for Callista to answer.

"We were able to get to him in time. He's snoring away in one of the kennels now. They're going to keep him for the afternoon to be sure he doesn't go into anaphylaxis again. I wanted to tell you guys what happened and to ask if you wouldn't mind telling anyone who shows up at the property, we're on our way. We'll stop in town to have copies of the keys made and should be there within the hour."

"Honey, consider it done. We were headed there ourselves to see where we could help out. Give Gunnar a big hug from us. Zach too." She disconnected the call and wiped away the stray tears.

"Gunnar did that on purpose."

"Why would you say that? He almost died."

"Jess said Callie has had anxiety attacks at the thought of walking into the veterinary hospital again. The sanctuary was a whole other ball of wax. Ten to one she didn't think twice with Gunnar. She assessed the situation and flew into action."

"That lines up with what I saw in her mind when she opened to me. Maybe you're right. Maybe this is exactly what she needed to prove to herself she isn't broken or damaged goods."

"Zachary would never describe her that way. To him, she is perfect."

"Isn't that how it always is with people in love. Perfection is all in perception."

"You're my perfection."

"Awww, babe. You're gonna make me cry."

He kissed her hand and brought it to his heart. "You are allowed to cry as long as it's happy tears. I love you and I'm damn well gonna tell you every chance I get. Get used to it."

"That goes double for you, mister."

"I think I can handle that. What would you say to making it official?"

Goosebumps covered her skin and her stomach fluttered. "As in?"

He wiggled his ring finger with the ring Tony had designed for them. "You, me, and Mark have our own commitment ceremony when we get through this crisis of course."

Even though they didn't need any legal ceremony to promise each other forever, it meant the world to her Ian would want that for the three of them. "You've been thinking about this for a while?"

"After hearing Hok'ee and Fiona's story it hit me hard. I want everyone to know the three of us belong to each other and pledge forever. Maybe that makes me a big softy, but I don't care. I want this and I'm going to make it happen."

She smiled. "Well then I'll make sure you get it. I love you, Ian Campbell."

"I love you, too Danielle Carson. Oh, that is going to change after we get married. We can pick something all three of us want as a last name."

She rifled through the glove box to find the travel sized Kleenex. "Damn you. Here come the waterworks."

He laughed and stomped on the accelerator as soon as he cleared Main Street and entered the highway. "I promise to make it up to you later."

Callista and Zachary arrived sooner than anticipated. She immediately got to work distributing keys to the buildings and the veterinary satellite clinic. Ian checked in with Chuck about coordinating additional crews to work on the construction of the housing for the animals. Danielle joined Zachary in the main house while he waited for his girlfriend to give him the grand tour.

"Jess is going to go apeshit over this kitchen. She'll be able to literally feed an army from here."

She placed her hand on his arm. "You don't have to show me around, love. How you holding up?"

He sighed and pushed his sunglasses on top of his head. "I've never been more scared of anything in my life, except when Jess told me Callie had overdosed."

"She said Gunnar will make a full recovery."

"Thanks to her. You should have seen her in action. I tossed his limp body over my shoulders and we ran into the ER next door. She yelled out what she needed and the techs flew into action. No questions asked. Boom. Catheter is in. Boom. More drugs administered. Boom. He's opening his eyes and wagging his tail. Damn dog cost me at least five more of my nine lives."

She hugged him and rubbed his shoulders. "He will give them all back to you with interest. That's his way."

"Can I ask you something?"

"Anything."

"Have you seen Jonah Hawkins around town lately? Both of us have been picking up his cherry tobacco pipe smoke and hearing his voice. Callie heard it on her hike yesterday telling her to let herself go and let the magic of Ouray heal her."

Danielle nodded. "I didn't know who he was at first, but I saw him when you brought Gunnar out to Taboo for the first time."

"So, he is connected to Gunnar. I knew it!"

"Trust your heart, Zach. You know the magic that's here. You know what I can do. In the coming weeks you're going to witness a hell of a lot more you thought were fairy tales. Believe and everything will become crystal clear."

"What the hell. Why not?"

"There's the spirit! You want me to stick around until Callie joins you?"

He shook his head. "I'm good. I think I'll hang out in the bedroom upstairs. She has a killer view from the wrap around deck."

"Don't you mean *both* of you will have this killer view? You know she wants you to move in her with her right?"

He smiled. "The thought had crossed my mind."

"Good. Do more than that and say yes when she asks you. The two of you deserve your happy ever after. This is part of it." She kissed him on the cheek and waited until he got halfway up the stairs. She opened the front door to find Ian leaning against his mustang.

"I hear some hot chick is in need of a ride home."

"I don't know. My fiancés may not appreciate some stranger dropping me off."

He smiled and pulled her into his arms. "As one of them I can safely say we wouldn't appreciate it if this stranger tried to have his way with you."

"Take me home, lover."

His lips brushed over hers in the butterfly kisses that set off the chain reaction that ended with her panties wet.

"As you wish…"

Chapter 15

Danielle double-checked the logs and compared them to the new inventory lists she had printed off in the morning. Sure enough, someone had been stealing supplies from Taboo's overflow storage area in the pole barns next to the house. Thankfully, none of the evacuation supplies had turned up missing.

"Who the fuck would take linens and uniforms?" She ran her fingers down the boxes stacked on the shelves and found three more had been opened and half of their contents removed. These open boxes caused the hair on the back of her neck to stand up. The missing garments were meant to be used for the new security details coming in. All had been embroidered with the names of each new employee. Five people—including herself—knew about these and she trusted all of them with her life.

That could only mean one thing…

The computer crash the week before had been no accident. Someone had hacked into their system before their IT guru was able to fix the damage. They hadn't thought twice about it since no evidence of a security breach with personal data of their guests had taken place. Whoever had been responsible wanted specific information about Taboo's security plans and ways to get inside without raising suspicion.

"Knock, knock!"

She turned and smiled. "What brings you over here, Zach? I thought you and my guys had plans to finish the barbecue pits."

"We polished those off this morning and ran them up to Jess. She wanted to start the fires now so the coals would be ready in time to feed the first crews. They're do back around six. I wanted to check in with you. Gunnar has been upset and barking his fool head off. Someone has been snooping around outside and he ran off when we pulled up. I left Gunnar in the truck to warn me if they come back around."

"You sure it wasn't one of the evac people?"

He shook his head. "Why would they run off? They're welcome on both of our properties."

"Good point. Someone has been in here since yesterday. I'm missing our new personalized security uniforms, sheets and towels. I'm not too upset about the linens, but the uniforms are another story. They're not only personalized with each employee's name but have tracking devices implanted in the material. After Gabe was locked in the freezer, we weren't going to take any more chances."

"Someone is desperate to get into Taboo as one of your employees. What the hell is going on?"

Mark and Ian walked through the open door. "I think I can answer that. Caron has been running his mouth all over town about making Callie pay for embarrassing him at the sanctuary."

Zachary stiffened and clenched teeth together. "He tries anything and he is a dead man. Even if this is his handiwork, why lash out at the three of you if he is out to get Callie?"

Mark sat on one of the stools stored against the nearby wall. "As you know, we've had problems with him since before we broke ground. It has been one thing after another with him. He seemed to drop his claim on this property, but he's been working behind the scenes to grab up your and Callie's. I looked further into the claims he has on your place and he was telling the truth about one thing. Berringer had promised him the town council would approve his plans to build an evac camp once he purchased the land. Without Theresa in the mix to stall the sale, he thought he finally won. Apparently, he planned to charge the people using the facilities. For the favor, he promised Berringer he would pay higher taxes and fees associated with such an enterprise."

Zachary shook his head in disgust. "Making money off of the misfortune of others is beyond reprehensible. I never thought I would see anyone in Ouray pull that kind of stunt."

Ian crossed his arms over his chest and leaned against the corner of the shelves in front of them. "I gave up trying to figure out why some people will throw their own family in harm's way if it means they can make a few extra bucks. You of all people know what goes into building all the structures out here. You know damn well if

Caron got his hands on these properties, he would skimp on materials and labor and charge up the ass to those looking for a safe place to ride out the fires."

Ian's emotions raged under the surface. He pushed off from the shelves and paced around the room. She reached out for his hand as he passed in front of her. He latched on and pulled her to him into a hug. He visibly calmed in her arms and kissed the top of her head. "Thanks, darlin'"

"Awww. Ain't that sweet? Mangy mutt had to be calmed down by the resident witch."

They spun around to find Caron in the doorway, dressed in one of the new security uniforms and a semi-automatic pistol in hand.

Ian moved her to stand next to Zachary and joined Mark circling the room toward Caron. Mark held his hands out, palms up. "I'd think twice about using that weapon, son. In the time it takes for you to shoot one of us, the other will have you gutted."

Caron shrugged. "You're not the only one who can handle a gun, asshole. I grew up with weapons. I didn't need to join the Marines to get my hands on one."

Mark mimicked the other man's shrug. "Fair enough. You still don't need a gun to talk. Why are you here waving one around?"

Ian's eyes changed from brown to gold and he emitted a low, deep growl. Caron swung the gun toward him. "Easy there Rambo. I'm done taking shit from all of you. It's *my* turn to talk and *you* listen. The Fire Queen said the three of you would try to pull a fast one on me but I assured her I could handle any wolf that crosses my path. I already took out dozens before you showed up."

Bile rose to the back of her throat. Their instincts had been right all along. Caron had been the one responsible for all the wolf orphans at the sanctuary. "Why is she so concerned with the wolves?"

He rolled his eyes at her as if he thought she was the most ignorant being he had ever met. "She had to be sure you never made your way back here. Keep the wolves out and the White Witch will never come into power. I guess she never counted on these two tasting your honey pot back in Nevada."

Ian and Mark tightened their circle, closing in and ready for action at the first opportunity.

Zachary moved to place his body in front of her, blocking Caron's view.

"I said, don't move! What the hell is wrong with you jarheads? I want a clear shot of all four of you in case anyone decides to be the hero."

She lifted her chin and concentrated on keeping her voice calm and even. "Please. Let Zach go. He has nothing to do with this."

"Like hell! He helped build this place. As far as I'm concerned, he's in it up to his eyeballs. I've got a whole other beef with him now. It's his girlfriend who fucked me over. Thanks to her stunt, I've lost my job and any hope of finding another one."

Zachary clenched his fists until all the veins on his arms stood up. His breathing became ragged in his attempt to reel in his fury. She placed her hand on his arm. "He's not worth it."

Caron laughed. "You banging him too? Must have a lot of fun fucking all three at once. Now you have a vet to cover all the medical help your body needs after whoring around with the likes of these cast offs from society."

Zachary's unblinking eyes locked on Caron. "I'd stop talking if I were you."

"Hero is out today and ready to roll! I was beginning to think you would keep yourself drugged up. Hawkins must be some piece of ass to get you out of that cabin of yours."

She threw her hands straight up to the ceiling and raised her voice in an incantation, not to complete a spell but to create a distraction. "I call upon the Goddesses Artemis and Athena—"

"Not today, Witch!" Caron swung his arm wildly toward her and lost his balance. In his attempt to right himself, he gripped harder on the gun and squeezed the trigger.

In her mind, everything ran in slow motion. She shoved Zachary to the floor as Ian and Mark shifted in mid-air. Their growls turned to snarls as they flew at the shooter. The bullets whistled through the air between them until their thudding impact with Black Wolf.

Not one peep out of him as he dropped to the floor on all fours, spun around and bared his teeth.

Caron violently shook his head. "No. It was an accident—"

Black Wolf had no intention of listening to another word. He and Gray Wolf lunged for Caron's throat.

The man screamed and shot at both wolves without aiming as he scrambled over the floor, desperate to keep from the vicelike jaws of her Guardians. One of the bullets ricocheted and clipped Gray Wolf in one of his forelegs, triggering his transformation back to Ian.

"No!" Her screams echoed throughout the building as Black Wolf swayed and fell to the ground in a lifeless heap."

Ian had been in full stride after Caron but froze at the sound of her scream. He spun around and sank to his knees, blood streaming from the wounds above his elbow and in his bicep. Caron used the opportunity to make his getaway.

Zachary's voice broke through to her. "Forget about him for now. Help me get Mark…Black Wolf into the back of my truck. We need to get him to the satellite clinic."

She sobbed and draped her body over her Guardian. "Hold on, help is coming. She'll do it right? Callie will meet us there?"

He nodded his face full of confidence in his ladylove. "She is the Guardian Healer of the Arrow. She will do everything she can to save him. Trust in her and in your magic."

She gulped several breaths and nodded. "Ian, I know you want to go after Caron, but we need you now."

"As soon as I know Callista is on her way…"

"I'll let you go with my blessing. There are sheets in the box against the wall. Cover the back of the truck with them."

Zachary jumped up to do as she asked, Gunnar glued to his side.

She turned back to Ian and gripped his hand. "Once we have him in there, we can cover him up. I don't want to freak anyone else out right now, especially the other wolves staying at Taboo."

"Let them loose, Dani! Caron deserves everything they'll do to him."

She shook her head. Not this way. If Caron is connected to Fitche, even remotely, she will use it as an excuse to push forward with the war. If it's one wolf, grieving for his partner, the rest of the Elders will see it our way."

"How the hell can you be so calm? Gray Wolf's howls are all I can hear."

"He cut me out for now to keep me from his grief."

"Truck is ready and no one is around." Zachary brought a sheet of plywood to use as a gurney. Black Wolf raised his head and looked into Zachary's eyes.

"I trust you with my life and that of my clan. Gunnar was wise to wait for you to come along."

Zachary gasped and reached for the end of the gurney. "Did he really speak to me?"

Ian lifted the other end and smiled through his tears. "That he did. It's an honor he gifts to very few humans."

She glanced between the two men as they loaded Black Wolf into the truck. Both appeared to put on their Marine faces, keeping all emotions out and concentrating on the task at hand. This is what she would be facing in the coming days if the Unseelie Queen forced a war.

"You sit up front with Zach and Gunnar. Try to reach Callie. I'll stay with him back here."

Zachary punched the speed dial on his phone's screen and handed it to her to hold as he concentrated on getting over the bridge between their properties without attracting any more attention.

"What's up, babe?"

"We have an emergency here at the satellite. I don't want to get into it on the phone."

"I'll send a team."

"Callie? This is Dani. You have to come alone. It's one of my wolves."

The silence on the other end nearly sent her into a panic. "I don't understand."

"Don Caron shot my Black Wolf. He shot Mark. Please, Callie. He's lost a lot of blood."

"I'm on my way."

She tapped the button to disconnect the call. Tears steamed down her face. She thanked the Goddess for bringing both Zachary and Callista into their lives. Without a doubt, she would lose their chance to save Mark and Black Wolf without access to medical care for them. Human hospitals and paramedics wouldn't have a clue how to treat either of them. At least in Ouray she had access to Shaman and other healers.

"Shaman will be back this afternoon."
"You let me back in, thank you."

"I didn't block you, darlin'. Black Wolf asked to keep you out of our heads until the danger has passed."

Figures. Even now they kept things from her. She vowed to give all four of them holy hell once she knew Black Wolf and Mark were okay. She refused to let even the suggestion both wouldn't make a full recovery into her mind or her heart. If she did, then she would have to admit she didn't want to live if either Mark or Ian were ripped from her. She had spent her entire life searching for them. She kicked herself for not taking Ian up on his suggestion to run away from all of the chaos.

"Stop. We're all in now, even Black and Gray. None of us are going anywhere without the others."

"I love you, Ian. I know you have to go after Caron but please promise to come back to us."

"Nothing and no one will keep me from coming back. I love you, too. I wouldn't leave him if I didn't know Callie will do everything she can to save him."

Zachary brought the truck to a skidding stop at the back door of the clinic. He handed her his keys and grabbed his end of the makeshift gurney. "The blue utility key will open the door. We need to get him into the surgery suite. Callie will be here as fast as her jeep will fly through town."

Her hands shook as she slid the key into the slot and held the door open. Black Wolf emitted a soft whine that nearly split her heart in two. She flipped on the light in the surgical suite and gasped at the amount of equipment they had in the facility. She wasn't a doctor, but it looked like Callista would have everything at her fingertips to help her Guardian.

"We're going to lift you off the board and move you to the table. Try not to move on your own, Black Wolf. Your wounds will start to bleed again." She knew Ian spoke out loud more for Zachary's benefit than for his companion. Truth be told, his voice helped to calm her too.

The beast groaned as they shifted his enormous body to the stainless-steel table covered with circulating water blankets. Ian rested his forehead against his partner and buried his hands in the black mane. "Justice for you both."

She expected to feel the worry and the fear, but the ice-cold fury caught her by surprise. She wanted Ian to catch the bastard and make him pay. Her eyes locked with Ian's as he backed away from the table. Gray Wolf howled in her mind, ready for the hunt.

Zachary brought her one of the stools from the far wall and excused himself keep his eyes out for Callista. She rested her cheek on Black Wolf's head and draped her arm around his neck. "Callie will be here any moment and we'll have you back running in no time. Rest now."

She heard voices and Gunnar's soft wolf at the front of the clinic and sobbed in relief. She looked up to find Callista staring wide-eyed at the scene in front of her. Danielle's emotions ran too high for her to concentrate on reading the other woman's thoughts. She detected a faint cherry tobacco scent in the room and a deep baritone voice.

"You know what to do, Guardian. Trust in yourself."

Danielle's eyes stayed on Callista's face as it appeared to change from confusion to calm determination. "Ian went after Caron. That bastard better pray he doesn't catch him. Ian will rip him apart."

Callista nodded in agreement. It appeared to her that she accepted the fact Ian and Mark were shifters. She should have confided in her sooner than this, but here they were.

"Does he have any allergies or reactions to drugs that I need to be aware of?"

She shook her head. "He'll burn through anesthetic faster than a human."

Callista ripped open drawers and cabinets and gathered her supplies. "Zach, I'm going to need you to run his anesthesia. You'll have to give it to him in pulses to stay ahead of his system."

"Got it." He picked up the clippers and shaved both of the wolf's front limbs. Danielle assumed he had seen that done when they had rushed Gunnar in to the veterinary ER after wasps had attacked him.

She sat up and moved away from the table to provided Callista room to asses her patient for entry and exit wounds. Her sigh of relief encouraged Danielle. "Looks like the bullets passed through him. Once I get the catheters in, we'll snap a quick x-ray to confirm."

Danielle nodded. "What do you want me to do?"

"Put on the x-ray gown and switch on the unit. It's the big orange button on the front panel."

Callista lifted one of the stethoscopes from the hooks next to the prep area and listened intently to Black Wolf's heart and lungs. She appeared to be satisfied with her findings and looped the instrument around her neck.

Her patient whimpered and turned his head toward her. His golden eyes gazed into hers. Danielle stood transfixed by their exchange. First Zachary and now Callista had gained her Guardian's trust.

"Mark trusts you and so will I. My life is in your hands, Guardian Healer."

"Holy shit!" Callista's eyes filled with wonder and amazement.

She smiled. "He never speaks to anyone outside of our circle. Both of you are part of it now."

Callista looked to Zachary. "You can do it, sweetheart. This is who you are."

While it seemed an eternity to her, Callista moved swiftly and efficiently from preparing the wounds for exploration and cleaning. She talked throughout every step so both Zachary and Danielle knew what to do. She snapped off her first set of surgery gloves and slipped on the new pair set out. She had explained it was her way to minimize contamination throughout each stage of repair.

"It looks like one of the bullets nicked his axillary artery. I'm going to have to extend the wound edges to get better access to tie it off. Dani, I'm going to hand you a bulb syringe and a bowl of sterile saline so you can flush the wound. Don't worry if it spills over. I have suction ready to go to remove the fluid. It's important we keep it up until we are ready to close. Okay?"

"Got it. Gentle stream where you tell me to put it and you'll suck up the excess."

Callista smiled. "You got it."

Zachary continued the pulses on the syringe delivering the anesthetic. He kept Black Wolf under and pain free throughout the procedure. The rest of the surgery turned into a blur. One moment several clamps protruded from three wounds and the next, Callista had placed the last of her neat cruciate sutures.

"I'll put the bandages on after he shifts back to human form, if he still needs them."

Danielle pushed away from the table, hugged her and cried. "Thank you. Mark and Ian are my life."

Callista's eyes sparkled with unshed tears. Danielle had sensed how freighted she had been to see the wolf in her clinic. While she was not able to read her mind then, she could now. The steady stream of amazement they had saved another life, a shifter no less, told her Mark and Black Wolf's lives weren't the only ones saved that day.

"Once he's awake, we'll move him up to the house. Until Ian returns, I don't think it's safe at your place. The resort is swarming with evacuees and first responders, and yet Caron managed to get through and hold us at gunpoint."

Callista agreed. "Please stay here with us tonight. I'll be able to monitor him easier and intervene if he has any complications."

A soft rustling in the hallway drew their attention. Ian leaned his six-foot frame against the open door, his clothing in tatters. He crossed the room in three strides and caught Danielle as she leapt into his arms. "She saved them, Ian. Black Wolf and Mark will be fine."

"Words cannot express how grateful I am to you for caring for him."

Callista's brows furrowed and she touched the wound on his shoulder and the now healing wounds on his bicep. "Are you hurt?"

He shook his head. "It's almost healed. I'll be fine."

Zachary stared him in the eyes. "And Caron?"

"Sheriff has him in custody. He turned himself in blubbering about werewolves taking over the world. He'll try to plea insanity to get out of jail time."

Callista snorted. "Won't help. By the time my lawyers get done with him, he'll wish you had ripped him apart."

Ian lifted his eyebrows. "Is that so? Do tell."

She waved him off and smiled. "Forget about him. Now that you're back, you can help us move my patient to the house. Don't even try to argue with me."

Ian grinned. "Wouldn't dream of it, darlin'."

*

Callista examined his shoulder with a critical eye. One by one the sutures had fallen out as his muscles and skin knitted together. This was something he considered old hat, but he enjoyed the wonder in her eyes as the scar faded away as if it never existed.

"Fascinating."

"You're not so bad yourself, Doc."

Her eyes moved from his shoulder, over his bare chest and finally focused on his eyes. "Still feeling the effects of the alfaxalone?"

Mark knew damn well it wasn't the drug in his system causing his pupils to dilate. Having the hot vet this close to him, her vanilla and sandalwood scent tantalizing his senses brought all sorts of images to his mind on what they could do together. If Zachary hadn't been in the picture, he would ask Callista to be their fourth. "Not enough to keep me here in bed, unless you want to switch roles? I'll be the doctor and you can be the patient."

She blushed and rolled her eyes.

He smiled and kissed her cheek.

"Dude, stop flirting with my girlfriend while I'm in the room."

"Well, what do you expect? I wake up to find a beautiful woman hovering over me and I'm supposed to hold my tongue? I can think of better ways to put it to use."

Callista and Danielle laughed. "Knock it off you two. I think you've boosted my ego enough for a lifetime."

Danielle entwined her fingers with his. "What do you say, Callie? Is he clear to help out Jess with the barbecue?"

"As long as you promise to let me know if you feel any pain or weakness. The bullet nicked a major artery. You may heal like lightening, but I'd rather not take any chances."

He crossed his fingers over his heart and held up his pinky. "Deal"

Callista linked her pinky with his and grinned. "You might want these."

He took the clothes Ian had brought over for him and rested back against the pillows. He closed his eyes and connected with Black Wolf to be sure he was resting. Satisfied with what he saw, he opened his eyes again as Danielle climbed into the bed and into his arms.

"Sweetheart, why are you shaking?"

"We thought…I thought I was going to lose you."

He tilted her face up so she looked in his eyes. "I love you. Nothing will keep me from you. Not even death."

She shook her head. "Don't say that. Gift of the Elders or not. Death can take an immortal too."

"I refuse to believe the three of us will ever be ripped apart now we've found each other and no I'm not saying we can't die. Shaman shared with me more of our story."

"Why only with you?"

He shrugged. "I've been worried all of this is too much. Maybe the three of us are not meant to save Ouray or restore balance to the Realms. We, all three of us, are much older than we've been led to believe."

"I don't understand. I thought those memories of our past lives were given back to us once we mated. Are you saying we've continued to live throughout each generation of our families?"

He nodded. "Once we reached adulthood, our aging process sped up or slowed down depending on what we needed to accomplish. If we hadn't found each other by a specific point in our life stage, we would go through a rebirth."

Her eyes widened. "Like a phoenix? Like my father?"

"And your uncles."

"Seamus and Cael are no family to me. They've made their positions perfectly clear."

"Aidan risked his life to find you again. He came to Ouray to protect you from Fitche. He wasn't about to let that wench take you from him too."

"Who else has she taken besides my parents?"

"I don't know their whole story, but Rain and Aidan had been very much in love. He had planned on giving up his gift to be with her."

She appeared confused. "Uhm. The last time I checked, Rain had gone from being repulsed by him to being in love with him again. The two of them confuse the hell out of me."

He laughed. "I told you I don't know their whole story, but Shaman said they'll find their way back to each other when we need them the most."

She rolled her eyes. "Riddles again?"

"You and your aunts don't corner the market on them you know." He pulled her back into his arms. She rested her head on his shoulder. This is what he wanted to do since he woke up. Ian wasn't the only one who calmed in her arms.

"I know. I promise to make every effort not to fall into that habit. We've had too many riddles blocking us from finding each other. Straight talk from here on out. Except with my spells. They sound cool when they rhyme."

Her giggle tickled his heart. He and Ian had promised each other they would make sure to give her a moment to laugh or smile each day. With the addition of Callista and Zachary to their tribe, he hoped those moments would build and grow.

Our lives are not our own right now, but that's as it should be. It's the only way we're going to stop Fitche from destroying everything in her path.

Chapter 16

"Jessalyn! Your grill masters have arrived."

Danielle laughed as her aunt stood in front of them with her hands on her hips.

"No need to be screaming, Ian Campbell. I'm standing less than three feet from ya."

Mark grinned. "Don't mind him any, Jess. He's excited you're letting him do anything with the food."

She handed both of them Kiss the Cook aprons. "I'm trusting you with the racks of ribs. They're pretty saucy so put on the aprons to keep your shirts from getting stained."

"You know, Jess, we could go shirtless and forget the apron?" Ian snuck up behind her and kissed her on the neck.

"Oh, you! Stop trying to distract me from my work with your muscles and tattoos." Her cheeks turned a flattering shade of pink and she fanned herself.

"What? And give up flirting with my best girl? Never!"

Her laughter rang out bringing smiles to all within earshot. Danielle tied one of the aprons around herself as the mayor and his wife came in with multiple trays of macaroni and cheese, lasagna and garlic bread as well as four pans of homemade brownies. Her stomach growled in response to all the aromas. The faster they set up, the faster she'd be able to sit down with the crews and enjoy the feast. These men and woman worked themselves to well beyond exhaustion to keep them safe. They deserved the hot food and down time they would receive that night.

She busied herself setting up the chafing dishes to keep the food hot. Thankfully all the donations had come in the form of the aluminum foil pans that fit into the warmers perfectly. Danielle joined Callista at the dessert table arranging all the sweets for easy access. Coolers stuffed with ice and cold drinks as well as a coffee and tea station were up and ready to go as the first of the crews arrived.

Jess's voice boomed out over the area. "Come on in and grab yourself a plate. We have tons of food and more will be out as it's ready. Don't by shy about grabbing seconds and thirds. Plenty to go around."

Cheers from the new arrivals made her smile. This is why they volunteered to help out tonight. If they could bring them ten minutes of down time and a cheer for hot food, then everything was worth it. They had lost contact with three of the hotshot crews and those coming back to camp were now hearing about it. One young kid, barely in his twenties sat on one of the benches next to his team leader. He dropped his equipment at his feet and covered his face with his hands.

Callista bumped her shoulder. "His brother is one of the missing."

She tried to shield herself from the raw emotions pummeling her from all directions. Their voices echoed in her head.

"Please don't let him be gone."

"Damn flames laughed at us. I swear I could hear the laughter echoing throughout the valley."

"They think we have an arsonist out there on top of this shit. Who the hell does that?"

"Missing? The whole crew?"

"Devon Ross is still out there." Callista sat down on the bench waiting for the next group to come up to the line.

"Lester's son? He the one who runs the hotshots out of Cali?"

"That's him. I used to babysit him and his sister when we were kids. It's all I can do to keep myself from asking if they've reported in yet. Darby is keeping herself busy too but I can tell she's about ready to vomit thinking the worst."

She hugged her friend. "Somehow he's going to get through it and be back with everyone who loves him. I can't explain it, but I have a feeling. I can't connect with him. Something is blocking me. That something is how I know he is alive."

"Thank you. I forgot how wildfire season could suck the life out of us. I'll be happy when this season is over."

"How much more do you have to do yet at the sanctuary?"

"Just Momma Lynx. Once she's out then everyone will be settled north of town. We're going to be inundated with evacuees from Durango and Silverton throughout the night and into tomorrow. Jack and Jess will follow up with Zach while I finish at the sanctuary. Once we're at the new house, we're staying put for the duration, barring any emergencies that is."

"Momma Lynx?"

"She was a last-minute arrival at the veterinary hospital. She had been shot and left for dead. Our surgeons repaired her wounds and found her pregnancy at that time of her surgery. I couldn't tranq her again and risk her kittens. Got word tonight she finally stayed in her den we made for her. They've secured the opening so now we can transport her at first light. I want her out of there before the heat hits and to avoid getting stuck in a slow-moving caravan. I can't risk her getting heat stroke after all we've been through with her."

"You look like you're dead on your feet. Go relax with Zach for a bit. I'm sure we'll be able to cover everything and clean up if you want to head over to the cabin. This way you'll be close and get an early start with the evac of Momma Lynx and your family."

"I promised to look after Mark."

"You saw for yourself that he's healing up fine. I love that you want to watch over him, but if anything happens, we have Rain and Hok'ee. Plus, I have you on speed dial now."

Callista laughed. "Good, I have you on speed dial, too."

She stood and pulled Callista up from the bench and directed her toward the table with Lester and the fire marshal. Zachary scooted over for her to sit close to him. The look on his face as she snuggled up to him, brought another smile to Danielle's face. That man deserved every moment of love and happiness Callista brought to his world. Together they would beat back their demons along with their trusted sidekick, Gunnar.

This Momma Lynx intrigued her. What were the odds that Callista would have a pregnant lynx in her care? Could she be Aithne finding her way back to her family? Once they had her settled in her new habitat, she would bring Aidan and Rowan out to see what they thought of her. If her hunch was correct, they may finally have the missing piece of the spell to summon Morpheus.

170

She stood to greet the next arrivals. "Welcome to the barbecue. We have something for everyone, hot and cold. More on the way out and the grills are loaded with ribs that will melt in your mouth. If you're too tired to take another step, sit yourself down and I'll be right over to give you a hand."

Ian and Mark saluted her from the positions at the grill. Darby ushered some to the tables and others headed right to the food line. As long as the firefighters came to them, they would be there to help fill their bellies. They had stopped taking reservations for the duration of the evacuations in order to keep the rooms open for the firefighters in need of a comfortable bed and a shower. Any of the evacuees needing a room would be provided one, free of charge. Tony and Lia had agreed with their decision to do this. Money could be earned at any time.

Lester tipped his cowboy hat in Callista's direction. "I was saying how impressed I was with how you took over the sanctuary, Callie."

"We still have Momma Lynx to move in the morning. She finally stayed in her den long enough to secure her inside. After that, we're headed out ourselves."

Lester nodded. "Good idea. With all of you in place, it will make it much easier for the residents to check-in and set up camp, or continue on until they can come back in. The sheriff will most likely send out the emergency alerts within the next two days with recommendations to take shelter."

"Frank, your crews are welcome to the bunk houses if they need them."

"Rooms at Taboo are open too."

Frank appeared overcome with emotion. "Tonight, was an unexpected reprieve thanks to all of you. I don't know how to thank you for your offers. I'll spread the word and make sure they take you up on it."

Ian dropped down in the seat across from Frank and Lester. "We'll come pick them up from camp if need be."

"At the rate the fire is moving, we may be busting out of here tomorrow with all of you and headed to a new location north of here."

"Still close enough for Jess and I to bring up hot meals."

Frank tapped his hand over his heart. "Dani, you have no idea how much that means to all of us out there."

She leaned into Ian and rested her head on his shoulder. "Ouray is our home and our family. You do everything you can for family, without question and without expectation of payment."

Jess joined them. "Damn straight. It's time they all know your connection here. Danielle is my niece and Rowan's granddaughter. She's been kept from us all these years and has finally come home to stay."

"I knew it!"

"You knew nothing, Jackson Hawkins. You can't go around asking everyone in town if they're a witch you know."

Lester threw his head back and laughed. "So much for keeping Ouray's magic a secret. Next thing you know, we'll be the setting for his next movie."

"Hey now! I've kept it under wraps this long. Why would I tell the world about it now?"

"Good point. I have to say the circumstances suck but having not one, but two Hawkins back in Ouray has been wonderful. Jonah would be proud to see what you've done here."

Callista reached for his hand. "Thank you. It's great to be back here for good. Jack on the other hand will leave us as soon as we're all safe again."

"I don't know about that. Ouray has been working its magic on me again too. In fact, Siobhan keeps putting the bug in my ear about settling down in anywhere but LA."

Jess covered her heart with both of her hands. "Don't tease me, Jack. I don't know if my heart can take it."

Danielle watched the exchange closely. As she watched them speak to each other, their hand gestures and facial expressions were all similar, if not exactly the same.

Callista and Jack are her blood relatives. She was sure of it.

Jess turned her eyes toward her and nodded.

"They don't know yet. I'd like to keep that secret a little while longer, at least until Jack moves back. Once both are safe here in Ouray we can tell them together."

"I would be honored to be there when you tell them."

He got up from the picnic table and hugged her. "I would never joke about something like that. I'm not about to fight to save my hometown and not live here again. I may need your help to convince a Siobhan Ouray is where it's at."

Danielle cleared her throat. "You might be surprised. I spoke to her a couple months ago. She said Ouray called out to here the last time she was here."

Jack tilted his head. "When was that?"

"She was my guest for our grand opening in January."

"That would explain all the brochures she conveniently left all over my house and office." He winked. "I think I've been had."

The table erupted in laughter. Even with all the chaos around them, they managed to find something to bring a laugh or smile to each other's faces. She kissed Ian and excused herself to start condensing the food into smaller areas and helping create packages for those too tired to eat now. She made them promise to come up to Taboo or the ranch bunk houses on their off time. Three of the crew asked for nothing more than a hug from her. They missed their families back home and craved the touch of another human. She held on for as long as they needed.

The last one in the hug line was the young man she had seen crying on the bench. His grief washed over her and almost pulled her under. He launched into her arms and sobbed. His heart broken into a million pieces at the realization he had lost a brother and a sister to the Million Dollar Fire.

"I'm coming for you, Fitche."

Chapter 17

Danielle didn't recall seeing her aunt so upset, except after Callista had been hospitalized. Jess had to sit down to catch her breath and wipe away her tears. She handed the older woman a glass of cold water. "It's okay, honey."

"I can't believe I didn't see the steamer under her desk. I was so fixated on packing her other things, I didn't think."

She knew the steamer held letters from Jonah Hawkins to Callista. As precious as they were for her friend, Danielle knew without a doubt Jess saw them as a piece of one of the great loves of her life. "It's not your fault, Aunt Jess. I'm sure Callie double checked before she left."

"If anything happens to those journals, I'll never forgive myself."

"Let me see if we can reach someone close to your house. They'll be able to grab it for us and bring it here on their way through."

The sound of Gunnar's woof reached her ears. She walked to the front of the house and peered through the bay windows to see Ian watching Zachary's truck move down the winding driveway toward the highway. "Ian? Where's Zach off to now? Callie is going to flip if he's not here."

"He promised to be back before she walks through the front door."

"Oh, shit. The golf cart is out back. I bet he overhead us talking about Callie's steamer."

"The one with the journals?"

She closed her eyes and nodded. Her shoulders drooped. "He's been barely holding it together today and now he's headed back into that mess. What if he has an attack and can't get back here?"

Ian pulled his phone out of his pocket and sent out a mayday to his crew scouting the area near Tailwind and in town. "I should have gone with him. Fire and Rescue has their hands full right now. No one has heard from Cal since he left Taboo yesterday morning and Darby was trapped in the hiking trails behind Tailwind."

"What? Is she okay?"

"Black Wolf was able to show her the way out. Mark, Jenson and Carter are leading another set of wolves in search of the hotshot crew trapped in Box Canyon."

"Cal can handle himself and take care of his guide too. I know he wants to find himself up here but getting himself trapped between these fires isn't going to do any good. Maybe we should send out more help."

"Already on it." He tipped his phone toward her to show the recipients of his May Day.

Aidan and Siobhan. If anyone could sweep the area faster than the others it would be a phoenix and an angel.

*

Ian moved the golf cart back to its spot in the barn and hooked it up to the charger. He'd been amazed at how long the battery had held up over the last two days. He made a mental note to look into getting a couple of them for Taboo. As he approached the deck, he heard Jess's voice.

"This can't be happening. Not now. Both of them have come so far together."

"Gunnar's not the only one to pick up on his anxiety. Mark and I have been feeling it all day. He's struggling."

He looked up to see Callie standing there. "I'm going with you."

Jack spun around. "Going where?"

"Back to the main house. He went there for me, Jack. To get the journals. I can't not go after him. What if—"

Ian took the keys from her hand. "Come on, darlin'. Let's go get your man."

He maneuvered her jeep through the break in the traffic and shifted the gears as fast as the engine would allow. With the windows down, he heard the planes and helicopters flying overhead to drop their loads of water and flame-retardant slurry on the inferno racing through their mountains. He glanced in Callista's direction. All color had drained from her face.

He gripped her hand in his. He knew without a doubt Zachary had put himself in danger of a full on catatonic episode for her. He would give his life to keep her happy. Her body language told him she had come to the same conclusion. Big lug forgot that the he's the one thing that makes her happy. Without him, she would be lost.

Like he would be without Mark and Danielle.

He stomped on the gas pedal and careened through the last mile of tree-covered road to the house. As soon as the jeep skidded to a stop, she bolted from the vehicle screaming is name. Gunnar's head showed in the open window next to the front door.

He whistled for the group of firefighters to send over the medic and ran through the open door after her. He sprinted up the stairs to find both of them on the floor of her closet. Zachary's entire body glistened with sweat. Gunnar licked his face and whined. "Is…Is it clear?"

He knelt down beside them and checked Zachary's bounding pulse. "I'll see what's keeping that medic."

He raced back down the steps in time to see the medic leaping onto the front porch loaded with his gear. "Is he conscious?"

"Yes, but he may be mixing his past with the present." Ian led him back to the room where Callista had managed to get Zachary out of the closet and sitting up on the bed. The way he clung to her spoke volumes. She was his anchor to reality now. If there was anything at all that proved to him they were soul mates; that was it.

The medic examined Zachary from head to toe. He placed an ice pack over the back of his neck and fixed the oxygen mask on his face. "This is the worst one I've seen you have, brotha. I'll need you to hold tight until your heart rate levels out. We'll have you out of here before you know it."

That was his cue to make himself scarce. He picked up the trunk and her grandfather's walking stick. The magic contained within it warmed his palms. The scent of cherry tobacco pipe smoke filled his nostrils. He glanced down at Gunnar and followed the dog's gaze back in the closet. There stood a smiling vision of an elderly man who had to be the famous Doctor Jonah Hawkins.

"Thank you, Guardian of the White Witch. Ouray has waited so long for all of you to return. The circle is complete."

"I don't understand. What circle? Please don't talk in riddles. You know how we hate that."

"No riddles. Get back to safety and the way will be clear. I promise."

He nodded. *"I'm gonna hold you to that, Doc."*

Callista sat in the backseat with Zachary's head in her lap. She smoothed his hair away from his forehead and told him over and over again how much she loved him.

Ian blinked away the tears from his eyes. If they had been delayed any longer, they could have lost him. Gunnar nudged his arm and licked his hand on the stick shift. "I'm good, buddy. I'm relieved everyone is okay."

Gunnar turned to look in the backseat and then settled his head on Ian's arm. Ian's own anxiety dropped even further. He shook his head and grinned. Nobody could get anything by the furball.

Jack met them in the driveway. "Jess has already staked her claim in the kitchen. Don't let her fool you. She's been worried sick about both of you."

She hugged him. "But not you, right?"

He smiled. "I might have puked a few times when I couldn't reach you."

"Your secret is safe with me. Can you help us bring Zach into the house? He's still a bit wobbly."

"It's not as bad as it was. Point me in the right direction." He slid over the seat and stood next to her. With each step he appeared to grow stronger and stronger, but half way up the walkway he stumbled. Gunnar barked and Jack caught him before he toppled over.

"I'll unload the jeep. You go ahead inside."

She wrapped her arms around Ian's neck and hugged him. "I don't know what I would have done without your help. You guys free for dinner? I'm sure Jess has prepared enough to feed an army."

He grinned. "Dani's already inside giving her a hand. Mark's hanging out in your main room with the rest of the guys from group. They're eager to meet you."

She smiled. "When I first moved back, I had hoped to stop by your club. You know, check out why the old farts in this town have their panties in a bunch."

"Darlin', you and Zach are welcome to Taboo any time. Say the word and you'll have the VIP treatment. I'm forever in your debt for what you did for Mark." He kissed her and shooed her toward the house. He watched her make her way up the pathway to the front steps and hesitate at the door. The sound of Zachary's laughter brought her out of her trance and she opened the door.

Ian grabbed supplies from the back of the jeep and stacked them with the rest of the items in the garage. He hauled the steamer and Jonah's walking stick inside and placed them next to the fireplace, out of the way of traffic, but where Callista would be able to find them. He joined the others in the living room as their group leader, Chuck stood to speak.

"I want to say an extra thank you to Callista and her brother Jack for spearheading the evacuation of the animal sanctuary. Of course, it goes without saying we wouldn't have been able to move everyone out of town in record time without the leadership of our very own Mayor Ross. Between this estate and the acreage at Taboo, we have a safe place to ride out the fires."

Lester raised his glass and draped his arm around his wife, Matty's shoulders. "To Ouray!"

"Ouray!"

Callista sat down next to Zachary and buried her face against him. He'd known her long enough to figure out she wasn't comfortable being the center of attention for very long. Zachary had confided in him he had planned on proposing to her that night, but with all the commotion, Ian wasn't sure Zachary would go through with it.

Until he slid from the couch down to one knee in front of Callista.

"Jess! You better get out here!" Jack moved to stand next to her seat on the couch.

"You don't have to scream like a banshee, Jackson Hawkins. I'm not deaf...oh, my!"

Danielle rushed out of the kitchen. He caught her hand and Mark held on to the other.

Zachary smiled and kept his eyes locked with Callista's.

"I love you. I've always loved you. Don't ask me how I know, but in each and every lifetime I have loved you and I'm damn sure I'm going to love you in the next. You've been with me through one of my worst moments and you stayed. I told you I won't ever let you go again and I meant it." He presented a red velvet ring box to her in the palm of his hand.

She covered her mouth with her hands, afraid she'd scream and drown out the rest of his speech.

"Life with me won't be easy, but I can promise you it will be filled with love. Will you do me the honor of spending eternity with me?"

A woof broke the silence.

"And Gunnar?" He sat next to Zachary, his eyes trained on her face, his body quivering in anticipation.

"Yes. Yes. Yes!" She threw her arms around both of them and cried. Happy tears this time.

Zachary opened the box. "This was my mother's ring. Before she died, she gave it to me in the hope that one day I'd give it to the woman who completed my heart and soul."

"Damn, I'm a sucker for the mushy stuff."
"We know. That's why Dani and I love you."
"Jonah is here, near the fireplace. Can you smell the cherry tobacco?"
The three of them turned to find the ghost grinning from ear to ear.

"They're together now because of you. Thank you, White Witch and Guardians. I'm forever in your debt and will do what I can to help bring the Circle together."

Danielle pulled them into the kitchen as the rest of the group dispersed to give the couple a few moments alone. "He's right. I know where the missing piece is."

"What are you talking about? I thought everyone was here now. Well, Jack still hasn't a clue Siobhan arrived this morning, but we'll remedy that tonight." Mark waited for her to go on.

"Momma Lynx is here in her new habitat with six new babies."

He gasped. All this time her mother had been hiding in plain sight. If it really was her. "How can you be sure?"

"I overheard her caretakers today. She is one of the largest females they have ever seen and she gave birth to an unheard-of litter of six. In the wild they are known to have a maximum of four. Plus they're born during one of the worst fires we've had here in over a century. Aithne means fire. Don't you see? This is another sign. We have to gather everyone up. The full moon is in five days."

"What are the three of you doing in the corner whispering? We have an engagement to celebrate." Jess narrowed her eyes over her reading glasses. He had been on the recipient of that look more times than he could count and he loved it. Of course, he would never admit it to her. She would withhold it from him to get him all riled up. That's how they teased each other and why he adored her so much.

"We're plotting to take over your kitchen, that's what." He put up his hands in anticipation of her whacking him with her dishtowel. Instead she rolled her eyes and smiled.

"You tell me when and where, and I'll have my clan there ready for battle."

He kissed her full on the lips. "Woman, you amaze me."

"Oh, you devil! Kiss me like that again and you'll have to put a ring on it!"

"Don't think I won't!"

She slapped him with her dishtowel and walked back out into the living room.

"Should I be jealous of this other woman?" Danielle slid her own glasses down the bridge of her nose and narrowed her eyes in his direction."

Mark snorted and put his hand over his mouth to keep from speaking or laughing out loud.

Ian's body tingled all over. "You know what that look does to me, darlin'. I can't keep my hands to myself."

She squealed as he buried his face between her tits. "Come on, lovers. I'd like to sleep in our own bed tonight. We have a shit ton of work to do tomorrow to get ready to kick Fitche's ass out of Ouray."

"Sorry to break up the hug-fest, but could one of you show me where I can find Jack?" Siobhan wrapped her arms around them and grinned.

"He should be in the next room congratulating his sister on her engagement. I thought you wanted to wait until morning to surprise him."

"Aidan and Rain convinced me not to wait. All of us have put our happiness on the back burner long enough. I don't know what tomorrow will bring but I do know I want to spend every minute of every day with Jack."

"Did I hear my name…" He appeared too stunned to speak. Instead he darted across the room, held her face in his hands and kissed her breathless.

"Must be something in the air." Mark smiled and slipped his arm around Ian's waist along with Danielle's.

Jack smiled as he ended the kiss and turned to the three of them. "Have you been hiding her out at Taboo all this time?"

Ian shrugged. "Not exactly. Why don't we let Von fill you in? I'm sure we'll be seeing both of you at the farm house tomorrow."

Siobhan nodded. "We'll be there" She blew them a kiss as Jack led her out to the living room to introduce her to everyone.

Danielle placed her hand over his abs. "I've never seen her like this. She's positively glowing."

He kissed her forehead. "I have it on good authority that love will do that to you."

"Love is what will defeat the Fire Queen. It's something that has always eluded her."

"Will we really be able to defeat her this time, Doc? She's found a way to block us at every point so far."

Jonah opened his hands and gestured for them to look around. *"You have all you need here and in those who are gathered on these hallowed grounds. Families of Ouray have been reunited. Now is your time. At the height of the Full Moon as White Witch has already planned.*

She bowed her head toward Jonah. *"My heartfelt thank you for all you've done for my family while I was away. I wish I would have known you growing up. Jack and Callie are blessed to have had you then and now."*

"No regrets, Little Lynx. You have me now as well."

Jonah's ghostly form faded into the wall behind them leaving a trace of his cherry tobacco pipe smoke. Gunnar padded into the room, sat down and stared at the spot where Jonah had been. He turned to the three of them and winked.

Chapter 18

Rowan sighed. "What if you're wrong, honey? I don't know if my heart could take it if this is another dead end."

Aidan squared his shoulders and took her hand. "Come on, love. We've waited this long and searched high and low. What harm will it do if we take a look? At the very least we'll get to check out six new fluff balls."

Danielle took Rowan's other hand. "Callie will be there too in case our visit upsets Momma and her brood."

They drove Taboo's new golf cart over the stone bridge and across the gentle hills to the forest cat's new habitat. She parked their vehicle outside the entrance and waved to the volunteers at the door. "Doctor Hawkins is inside waiting for you."

She nodded and ushered Aidan and Rowan into the temperature-controlled unit. Low mewling and tiny growls grew louder as they approached the den. Callista reached for her hand and pulled her close to the rail. "Your timing couldn't be better. They're nearly done feeding. She'll show her face any moment now."

Danielle's body trembled in anticipation. She wanted to send out a telepathic message but wasn't sure if it would work. Aithne had been in her lynx form for nearly five decades, or longer if what Mark told her about their lives turned out to be true.

As predicted, Momma Lynx poked her head out the front of the den. Her eyes zeroed in on Rowan. The creature stretched one leg and then the other front leg out into the pen. She appeared to be moving slowly so as not to disturb the now sleeping kittens. As the last inch of her tail left the den her body shimmered and shifted rapidly from lynx to human.

Rowan grabbed the railing. "Aithne?"

The Seelie Princess stood to her full height and opened her eyes.

They changed from golden amber to pale silver. "Mother?"

Callista gripped Danielle's hand. "That was amazing."

A lump formed in her throat preventing her from speaking. There in front of her stood her mother. She appeared no older than a woman in her mid to late twenties. Her hair a pale blonde with silver streaks and black tips. Her delicate bone structure and long body mimicked her lynx features.

Aidan opened the gait of the pen and stepped inside, careful not to disturb the little ones. He held out his arms. "You've come home, at last."

She blinked rapidly and stared into his eyes. "Aidan!" She jumped into his arms and wrapped her body around his.

His hand rubbed her back and smoothed down her hair as she clung to him and cried. "Hush now. You're safe here with your family."

Aithne lifted her head and looked over his shoulder. "Help me move out of here. The babes need their rest."

He lifted her over the top of the enclosure and set her on her feet next to Rowan. "Is it really you, my daughter?"

Aithne's fingers moved over Rowans face, her arms and her hands. "You're real. All of you are real."

Rowan pulled her daughter to her chest. "I hoped against all hope you were still alive. I never dreamed we would find you here in Callie's sanctuary."

Aithne nodded to Callista. "Guardian Healer of the Arrow. I am forever in your debt."

"Pleasure was all mine." She coaxed Danielle in front of her. "Say something to her."

"Danielle? Is this my Little Lynx all grown up?"

Aidan grinned. "That she is. Now we call her White Witch."

Her mother reached for her. "The Prophesy came to life in my daughter."

Danielle moved into her mother's arms and immediately felt at peace. The last part of her heart had been returned to her. Jonah had spoken the truth. They had three days until the full moon to bring Aithne up to speed and help her regain her strength.

Rowan turned her attention back to the den. "Aithne, how will you care for the little ones now that you've shifted back?"

Her daughter smiled. "The others will come for them tonight. I was merely their wet nurse if you will."

"My volunteers watched you give birth to all of them. How can they not be yours?"

"They belong to all the Lynx clans as they too are shifters. They are old enough for the others to continue their care and watch over them as they grow. I'll take them to the Lake where the Lynx Elders will be waiting."

"I need a margarita."

Danielle giggled. "We're going to need a couple pitchers of them tonight."

Aidan held out his arm. "Hold on to me as you regain your footing. A lot has changed since you've been in hiding. Your daughter's house is full of those who have known you before and many you've yet to meet."

"Would that include her Guardians?"

Rowan laughed. "You'll fall in love with both of them the instant you meet. Your Aunt Jess and Ian have a thing."

Aithne's light melodic laughter tickled her ears. "Is that so? Then they'll fit into our family just fine."

Callista walked out with them and flagged down the caretaker. She appeared relieved to learn they didn't have to come up with a cover story. "We've got it, Doc. This isn't our first shifter rodeo."

"How many times do you witness it before it gets to be old hat?"

"It's frickin' awesome every time." The volunteer beamed.

"Oh good. I thought I was the only one to see it that way!"

Danielle hugged her. "You've saved another of my—our family. This is one habit I'm happy you have."

"Me too. Hop in. I'll drive you over and pick up Zach. He and Gunnar have been working on expanding the storage area with Mark. Aidan can drive your cart."

She climbed into the front of the cart. "You're taking all this magic stuff in stride."

Callista shrugged. "Taking care of Black Wolf and Mark opened me up to accept all of it. I believed in everything growing up here. It's out in the world where we lose that. Jack and I are proof positive Ouray's magic never leaves you. It sits dormant until you're ready to believe again."

"We're going to need you and Jack for this last ritual. You still up for it?"

"Hell yes. I'm not giving up without a fight. I believe in you White Witch."

Her heart swelled with love and a surge in strength from Callista.

The Wolf Clans gathered and formed the Circle of Power and Protection as the White Witch cast her circle around them and all in between. She called upon the spirits of the North, East, South and West to join them in their battle against the Fire Queen. The winds swirled around her from all directions bringing with them smoke and ash.

"We gather at the points of the pentagram within the Circle of Power to join our magic and plead our case to the Gods and give us aide to fight the wicked creature known as Fitche, the Unseelie Queen, Daughter of Morpheus and Lilith, Fire Queen and Dragon Queen."

Danielle, Ian and Mark stood together at the point of the pentacle in the North. Rain and Aidan joined together to her right. Rowan, Aithne and Jess stood together to her left. The point across from Rain and Aidan stood Callista, Zachary, Jack and Siobhan. The final point stood Fiona and Hok'ee. All raised their hands to the sky as clouds parted and the moon rose to its peak.

The winds outside the circle she cast howled and screamed with rage. Fitche flew overhead as her dragon form, hell bent on ripping them apart herself. "You will not stop me, witch. I will destroy you and everything you hold dear. While you play with magic, Ouray burns!"

Rain's voice rang out over the wailing winds. "We call upon the Navajo rain god, Tó Neinilii to bring the water from the sky and extinguish the fires that have scarred Mother Earth."

Hok'ee and Fiona's voices joined together as one. "We call upon Coyote to have mercy on his People and bring the rains to wash away the Death and Destruction from the Fire Queen and her army."

Lightning flashed through the sky and thunder reverberated around them. In the center of the pentagram the Great Thunderbird landed. He faced Danielle and bowed. "I have been sent to help you take back what is yours."

Jonah materialized next to the great beast as did Phalen the Red. "I have come to restore order and banish Fitche forever."

Callista's voice joined in the prayer. "The Guardian's of the Arrow gather here to ask Fate to intervene on our behalf and protect all creatures great and small from Fitche's wrath."

Artemis appeared next to Phalen. "Fate has asked me to answer your prayer, Guardians."

Aithne, Rowan and Jessalyn voices cry out as one. "The Witches of the Seelie Court ask the magical balance be restored to Mother Earth by stripping the Dragon Queen of all her power and immortality."

Fitche roared. Her anger caused the sky above them to turn into a fireball of orange, red and yellow flames.

"I am the White Witch and ask Morpheus to hear our prayer for he alone has the power to destroy what he brought to life."

The sky above them swirled with fire and smoke. Aiden's flame surrounded Rain. Fiona's Purple light swirled around Hok'ee. Siobhan unfurled her wings and projected her angelic essence through the Guardians of the Arrow. The witches combined their power into a green light that shot up toward the sky.

All the beings within the center of the pentacle turned toward Danielle as her phoenix fire exploded out from her and brought all of them within the protection of the white flames. "So mote it be!"

All of the magic gathered within her circle combined with hers and knocked them to the ground. White Witch and her Guardians stood as conduits, aiming all the magical energy toward the sky.

"We hear you and grant your wish."

The sky appeared to open up in front of her eyes. Small drops of rain tapped against her skin. One, two, then a dozen at a time. The tiny droplets increased in size and number until they stood in a downpour. All turned their faces to the sky and cheered.

She turned to the center of their pentagram to see her mother reach out for her father. His phoenix fire engulfed her as they embraced one last time.

"I'll always be with you, my Little Lynx." He smiled as he and Jonah faded away together. The other creatures and gods followed and promised to return if needed again.

Ian and Mark held her between them as the rain came down hard enough to sting and bounce off the ground. She looked around at the others waiting for her direction. "Help me close the circle so we can take this celebration inside."

All of them moved to the center of the pentagram and joined hands in a circle around Danielle. She gave thanks to the spirits of the West, South, East and the North and released them from the circle. She thanked all who had joined them on their journey and released them from their oaths as their time together had come to an end. "The Circle is now open, but never broken. Our hearts will forever be entwined. We will remember this day as the time we stood together against the darkness and banished it from our world."

She held out her hands to Ian and Mark. "Anyone else feel like dancing in the rain?"

Mark smiled and kissed her fingertips. "Where you go…"

Ian brought her hand to his heart. "We go."

"In that case, take me home. I want to fall asleep in each other's arms listening to the rain come down. The only fire burning tonight is what we have between us."

"Now you're talking. Let's go completely off grid for the next couple days."

"I'm game as long as you do that sexy librarian thing with the glasses. You know what that does to me."

She laughed. "Have I told you today how much I love you?"

Both shook their heads and grinned.

"Show and Tell. My favorite game."

The End

ABOUT THE AUTHOR

Lia Michaels is one of the alter egos of bestselling poet and erotic romance author Tammy Dennings Maggy. With so many characters clamoring for their stories to be told, the job became a bit overwhelming for one Sassy Vixen to handle. Lia "volunteered" to explore the world of M/M erotic romance as well as ménage and continue with the virtual adult resort blog with her fantasy hubby Antonin (Tony) Michaels.

A best-selling author in her own right, Lia promises very few topics will be taboo. So be sure to look for more fantasy and paranormal tales from her. She'll leave the more contemporary stuff to Tammy and Stephanie Ryan but still encourage them to push the limits!

Connect with Lia

authorliamichaels.net
www.sassyvixenpublishing.net

Made in the
USA
Columbia, SC